She Just Wasn't The One-Night-Stand Kind Of Woman.

Rounding the edge of the old brick building, she looked up and saw Dan Mahoney. Arms folded across his chest, feet crossed at the ankles, he stared at her from across the lot, and even at a distance, Angela felt the power, the hunger, in his gaze.

Parts of her body struggling back to life throbbed and hummed with an electrical pulse. As she started toward him, her heels tapped loudly against the asphalt and kept time with the pounding of her heart.

He leaned toward her. "So, Angela," he said softly, his voice whispering along her spine. "Do we still have a date?"

One last chance to back out, she told herself. To forget about the craziness of what she'd been planning and go home alone. But she knew that he was exactly what she needed. What she wanted.

There would be no backing out.

Not tonight…

Dear Reader,

As we celebrate Silhouette's 20th anniversary year as a romance publisher, we invite you to welcome in the fall season with our latest six powerful, passionate, provocative love stories from Silhouette Desire!

In September's MAN OF THE MONTH, fabulous Peggy Moreland offers a *Slow Waltz Across Texas.* In order to win his wife back, a rugged Texas cowboy must learn to let love into his heart. Popular author Jennifer Greene delivers a special treat for you with *Rock Solid,* which is part of the highly sensual Desire promotion, BODY & SOUL.

Maureen Child's exciting miniseries, BACHELOR BATTALION, continues with *The Next Santini Bride,* a responsible single mom who cuts loose with a handsome Marine. The next installment of the provocative Desire miniseries FORTUNE'S CHILDREN: THE GROOMS is *Mail-Order Cinderella* by Kathryn Jensen, in which a plain-Jane librarian seeks a husband through a matchmaking service and winds up with a Fortune! Ryanne Corey returns to Desire with a *Lady with a Past,* whose true love woos her with a chocolate picnic. And a nurse loses her virginity to a doctor in a night of passion, only to find out the next day that her lover is her new boss, in *Doctor for Keeps* by Kristi Gold.

Be sure to indulge yourself this autumn by reading all six of these tantalizing titles from Silhouette Desire!

Enjoy!

Joan Marlow Golan

Joan Marlow Golan
Senior Editor, Silhouette Desire

Please address questions and book requests to:
Silhouette Reader Service
U.S.: 3010 Walden Ave., P.O. Box 1325, Buffalo, NY 14269
Canadian: P.O. Box 609, Fort Erie, Ont. L2A 5X3

The Next Santini Bride

MAUREEN CHILD

Published by Silhouette Books

America's Publisher of Contemporary Romance

To my cousins, Jimmy and Doris Semon, who showed us
just how beautiful Louisiana really is. Thank you for
everything, you guys. We love you.

SILHOUETTE BOOKS

ISBN 0-373-76317-4

THE NEXT SANTINI BRIDE

Copyright © 2000 by Maureen Child

This edition published by arrangement with Harlequin Books S.A.

® and TM are trademarks of Harlequin Books S.A., used under license.
Trademarks indicated with ® are registered in the United States Patent
and Trademark Office, the Canadian Trade Marks Office and in other
countries.

Visit Silhouette at www.eHarlequin.com

Printed in U.S.A.

Books by Maureen Child

Silhouette Desire

Have Bride, Need Groom #1059
The Surprise Christmas Bride #1112
Maternity Bride #1138
The Littlest Marine #1167
The Non-Commissioned Baby #1174
The Oldest Living Married Virgin #1180
Colonel Daddy #1211
Mom in Waiting #1234
Marine under the Mistletoe #1258
The Daddy Salute #1275
The Last Santini Virgin #1312
The Next Santini Bride #1317

*Bachelor Battalion

MAUREEN CHILD

was born and raised in Southern California and is the only person she knows who longs for an occasional change of season. She is delighted to be writing for Silhouette Books and is especially excited to be a part of the Desire line.

An avid reader, Maureen looks forward to those rare rainy California days when she can curl up and sink into a good book. Or two. When she isn't busy writing, she and her husband of twenty-five years like to travel, leaving their two grown children in charge of the neurotic golden retriever who is the *real* head of the household. Maureen is also an award-winning historical writer under the names Kathleen Kane and Ann Carberry.

IT'S OUR 20th ANNIVERSARY!
We'll be celebrating all year,
Continuing with these fabulous titles,
On sale in September 2000.

Intimate Moments

#1027 Night Shield
Nora Roberts

#1028 Night of No Return
Eileen Wilks

#1029 Cinderella for a Night
Susan Mallery

#1030 I'll Be Seeing You
Beverly Bird

#1031 Bluer Than Velvet
Mary McBride

#1032 The Temptation of Sean MacNeill
Virginia Kantra

Special Edition

#1345 The M.D. She *Had* To Marry
Christine Rimmer

#1346 Father Most Wanted
Marie Ferrarella

#1347 Gray Wolf's Woman
Peggy Webb

#1348 For His Little Girl
Lucy Gordon

#1349 A Child on the Way
Janis Reams Hudson

#1350 At the Heart's Command
Patricia McLinn

Desire

#1315 Slow Waltz Across Texas
Peggy Moreland

#1316 Rock Solid
Jennifer Greene

#1317 The Next Santini Bride
Maureen Child

#1318 Mail-Order Cinderella
Kathryn Jensen

#1319 Lady with a Past
Ryanne Corey

#1320 Doctor for Keeps
Kristi Gold

Romance

#1468 His Expectant Neighbor
Susan Meier

#1469 Marrying Maddy
Kasey Michaels

#1470 Daddy in Dress Blues
Cathie Linz

#1471 The Princess's Proposal
Valerie Parv

#1472 A Gleam in His Eye
Terry Essig

#1473 The Librarian's Secret Wish
Carol Grace

One

"No man has a right to be that good-looking," Angela Santini Jackson said, nodding toward a man standing on the opposite side of the room.

Her sister Marie Garvey leaned in close and whispered, "He is a hunk, isn't he?"

Hunk barely covered it. The man had to be six feet four inches of solid muscle. His cheekbones were sharp enough to draw blood, and his eyes were a pale, brilliant green that seemed to glitter in his deeply tanned face.

He looked, Angela thought, like the poster boy for a don't-let-your-daughter-near-this-man campaign. She smiled to herself. He looked her way, and their gazes locked. Embarrassed to be caught staring, Angela quickly realized she had two choices here—glance away quickly and pretend to be oblivious…or meet his gaze squarely and refuse to back down.

She went with the latter. After all, it was a free world. A woman should have the right to look at anyone she wanted to. Right?

A long minute or two passed in silent observation. All around them people wandered about the private dining room of the Bayside Crab Shack. Her youngest sister's rehearsal dinner was almost over, and now the wedding party and their guests had time to chat. She heard snatches of conversations without really registering them. She knew her sister Marie was talking to her, but her voice sounded more like an annoying background buzz than anything else.

All she saw, all she focused on, was him. His eyes. The way he stood in the middle of everything and yet separate and apart from the crowd. It was as if he was off in his own world and was drawing her in there with him.

She shifted slightly in her seat, fought down the rush of warmth that slammed through her, and still couldn't look away.

It was as if they were in one of those old movies, where the hero and heroine exchange glances across a crowded room and the rest of the world blurred as the director homed in on his stars.

And that wild thought was enough to break the

spell holding her. She smiled to herself, and as she did, one corner of his mouth quirked up in a tilted smile, and he lifted his beer bottle in a mock salute as if to call their silent staring competition a draw.

Angela swallowed hard, gave him what she hoped was a regal nod, and when he looked away, turned her attention back to the sister who had now resorted to nudging Angela's ribs with her elbow. "What are you doing?" she asked.

"Funny," Marie said, giving a quick look across the room at the tall man now talking to Gina's fiancé, Nick. "I was just going to ask you the same thing."

"What are you talking about?" Angela picked up a place card and used it as a minifan in a futile attempt to cool her still-heated blood.

"What exactly were you and Mr. Wonderful over there doing?"

She dropped the card back onto the table and straightened up in her seat. "We weren't *doing* anything," Angela said, though even she didn't completely believe that. For the few seconds their gazes had been locked, she'd felt something almost…electrical pass between them. Oh, my, she thought, and reached for her glass of wine. Taking a sip, she let the cool liquid slide down her throat and hoped the chill would ease the last of the heat still crouched inside her.

"Not what it looked like from where I'm sitting," Marie muttered.

"Get a new seat," Angela told her shortly. Then, in an attempt to change the conversation, she pointed to their youngest sister and said, "Look at her. She's practically glowing."

Gina Santini smiled up at the man who would by this time tomorrow be her husband, and Nick Paretti bent down to claim a kiss.

"She's happy," Marie said simply.

"I hope she stays that way," Angela whispered more to herself than to her sister. Then louder she said, "Still, it's hard to believe that Gina's getting married. It all happened so fast."

"Maybe it's contagious," Marie mused as she held up her left hand to study the white-gold wedding band on her ring finger. "First me, then Gina, then…" She slid a glance at the woman beside her.

"Oh no, you don't," Angela said and held up both hands, making a cross out of her index fingers as if trying to ward off a vampire. "The phrase 'been there, done that' springs to mind."

Marie huffed out a breath. "For heaven's sake, Ange, just because you picked a lemon in the garden of love the first time around, doesn't mean you'll do the same thing again."

"Thanks so much for that very pithy piece of advice," Angela said with a nod. "But if you don't mind, I'm staying out of that particular garden from now on."

It was an old argument, Angela told herself. One she had no interest in reviving tonight. If her sisters wanted to get married, she would wish them every happiness and hope to high heaven that their marriages turned out better than hers had.

Old memories rose up in her mind, and Angela quickly pushed them back into the black hole where they were usually stored. This wasn't the time to remember the pain and misery that had been her marriage. This was a night to hope and pray that Gina would be as happy as Marie was.

"Oh," Marie said suddenly as an old, familiar tune swelled out of the speakers tucked discreetly into the four corners of the room. "I love this song. Think I'll go find my handsome husband and force him to dance with me."

Abandoned, Angela leaned back in her chair and took another sip of her wine. It was times like these when she most minded being single. All around the room couples were paired off, talking or dancing or laughing together. Even her eight-year-old son, Jeremy, was busy talking to the only other child in the room, a little girl he might normally have avoided like the plague.

She smiled to herself as she watched him. The one precious thing to have come out of marrying Bill Jackson was this little boy. And for the pleasure of having Jeremy in her life, she would be willing to go through all of it again.

"Who's that smile for, I wonder?" a deep voice asked from beside her.

Angela started and glanced up into the green eyes

that now seemed somehow familiar. Okay, it was one thing to stare at him with the safe distance of a room between them. It was quite another to have him so close she could smell his cologne.

And, oh, boy, did he smell good.

She cleared her throat and sat up straight, guiltily clearing her mind as though he could look into her eyes and see just what she was thinking. "My son," she said, motioning toward the boy who was apparently explaining the proper batting stance to a very bored little girl.

"Nice-looking kid."

"Thank you," she said, and stood up, wanting to be on a more even footing than having to look up at him. Well, she thought, as she tipped her head back...and back...to meet his gaze, so much for that idea.

"You're Angela, right?" he asked, shifting his gaze back to her and giving her that lopsided smile again.

Her stomach dropped as she nodded. He knew her name. How? Who had he asked about her?

"I'm Dan. Dan Mahoney."

"Hi," she said, silently congratulating herself on her sparkling wit and conversational abilities.

"I work with Nick," he continued.

"You're a Marine."

He smiled again, and her toes curled. "Isn't everyone?" he asked.

"In this room," she conceded, "just about."

Of course, that was to be expected when the groom to be was a Gunnery Sergeant. Heck, even Nick's brothers, Sam and John, who had flown in for the ceremony, were Marines. And Nick's father was an ex-Marine, if there was such a thing—which she doubted, since most of these guys seemed to be Marine right down to their bones.

She slid a glance at the Paretti boys, as she'd begun to think of them. Three brothers with jet-black hair, pale-blue eyes and more muscles than any three men had a right to. And not a one of them did a thing for her.

"Angela?" Dan said, and she drew her attention back to the man standing dangerously close to her. This man, on the other hand, seemed to have some weird effect on her nerves.

"Would you like to dance?" he asked.

"Dance?"

"Yeah," he said, that smile firmly in place. "You know, moving back and forth in tandem to a specific rhythm?"

Well, duh. God, why was she being such an idiot? Had it really been so long since she'd spoken to a man? Good heavens, had she kept herself so locked away that a conversation with a handsome man could actually paralyze her?

Apparently so. She swallowed hard, sucked in a breath and forced herself to say, "I'd love to."

"Good," he said, taking her hand and heading

for the small patch of parquet tiles passing itself off as a dance floor.

Angela concentrated on the feel of her hand in his. Wow. It was really an amazing sensation. Flesh pressed to flesh. Warm, strong fingers folded around her own. She hadn't even realized just how starved she'd been for a simple touch. And now that she had, other parts of her body were demanding a little attention, too.

That thought even surprised her.

In the midst of the other dancers, Dan pulled her into his arms and started swaying in time to the music. He held her right hand in his left and kept it tucked close to his chest. She felt his heartbeat beneath her hand, and the steady, even beat of it calmed her even as it excited her. It had been too long, she thought, as she began to relax and follow his lead. Too long since she'd danced with anyone but an exuberant Jeremy. Too long since she'd felt the hard strength of a man's arm around her waist, the press of his body against hers.

"You're a good dancer," he said, and his breath brushed her ear even as his voice rumbled along her spine.

"Thanks," she said, pulling her head back in self-defense. She was way too close to him for comfort. "You're a good liar."

He laughed shortly. "Okay, so neither one of us is Fred Astaire."

Nope, this slow turn in a tight circle would

hardly qualify as great dancing, but Angela didn't care. It was way more than she'd had in years. "Doesn't matter," she said. "It's nice."

"Yeah," he said softly, letting his right hand smooth up and down her back, "it is."

Angela shivered, and her eyes closed as she savored the feelings he inspired in her. Oh boy. Maybe it hadn't been such a good idea, living like a recluse for the past three years. She was way overreacting to this situation.

"You're beautiful," he said.

Her eyes opened, and she stared up into those green eyes. If this was his regular line, it was pretty good. But it wouldn't do to let him know she was in desperate danger of falling for it. "And like I already said, you're a good liar."

"Not this time, lady," he whispered.

Her stomach flip-flopped, and her mouth went dry.

There was something happening here. Something that ran in a tense, hot undercurrent. The calm, rational side of her, the side that had had her in hiding for the past three years, was telling her to run fast and run far. The other side however, urged her to get closer. Urged her to enjoy this moment in time.

"Can I steal my sister for a minute?"

They both turned toward the woman speaking, and briefly Angela considered telling her little sister to take a hike. But something in Gina's eyes stopped her.

So instead, she reluctantly slipped out of Dan Mahoney's grasp and said, "Thanks for the dance."

"My pleasure, ma'am," he said, then gave her a slow wink before drifting off toward a cluster of Marines.

Sighing for opportunities lost, Angela turned to her sister and asked, "Okay, little sister, what's up?"

"Nothing yet, I hope," Gina muttered, glancing over her shoulder at Dan.

"What are you talking about?" Honestly, she loved her sister, but...

"Stay away from that guy," Gina blurted out.

"Excuse me?" She stared down at her sister in disbelief.

Muttering, "Come on," the younger woman grabbed her arm and dragged her across the room toward the open double doors leading to a brick patio.

A cool ocean breeze wafted into the room, and in the press of people, the chill was welcome. Stepping outside, Angela sent a quick look up at a star-filled sky, took a deep breath, then looked at Gina. "This had better be good."

"Nick says you should keep your distance from him."

"Oh, *Nick* says." Angela nodded and threw her hands wide. "Well, sure. Why didn't you say so?"

"Angie, he says that Dan's a nice guy, but he's

a one-night stand kind of man." Gina shook her head. "Not really the type for you, y'know."

Amazing. Her *younger* sister giving her advice on men, for heaven's sake. Although, she had to admit that Gina probably knew what she was talking about. After all, she'd already decided that Dan Mahoney was a smooth talker. But whether she listened or not should be up to her.

"How about you guys letting *me* decide who my type is?"

Gina pushed her hair out of her eyes, winced as if she knew she'd stepped into something, then tried to salvage it. "Nobody's telling you to do anything."

"You did," Angela reminded her. "You said to 'stay away from that guy.'"

"Okay, I put it badly, but I just wanted you to be careful...."

Careful? She hadn't been on a date, had in fact, hardly spoken to a man in the past three years. What could be more careful? For the first time in ages she was dancing with an attractive man, feeling those feelings she remembered so vaguely, and what happens? Her family comes so unglued you'd think she was a vestal virgin being slated for sacrifice.

Geez. If she wanted to do something daring...something out of character...something *dangerous,* wasn't she old enough to make that choice for herself?

"Gina—"

"Angela," her sister interrupted, "we've all been trying to get you back into the dating pool for years. I just don't want you to drown on your first time out."

She looked so concerned, Angela let her anger dissolve into nothingness. Reaching out, she pulled Gina into a tight hug then held her at arm's length and said, "Okay, I swear, if I start going down for the count, I'll give a yell, okay?"

Although right now the thought of drowning in Dan Mahoney's pale-green eyes didn't sound like such a bad idea at all.

Two

"**W**e ought to get together," Sam Paretti said. "Brother of the groom, sister of the bride...how perfect is that?"

Angela looked up at him and grinned. She couldn't help it. After meeting Nick's two brothers, Sam and John, she was willing to admit that the Paretti men were not only gorgeous, but charming, too. God had been on a real roll when he'd created these three.

"It's perfect, all right," she said, "heck, it's practically a romance novel."

"There you go," Sam said, and glanced toward the bride and groom. "They look happy, don't they?"

"Yes, they do," she said, watching her little sister dance with her new husband. Her wedding dress swirled around her in a froth of lace and tulle, and the smile on her face was bright enough to light the room. The man guiding her proudly around the dance floor looked handsome in his Dress-Blue uniform, and together they made an almost fairy-tale picture.

A pang of something sharp and bittersweet twinged around her heart. So much hope, so much love. Angela said a quick, fervent prayer that Gina and Nick would always be as happy as they were tonight.

Old tunes poured from the stereo system set up on the auditorium's stage. The church hall was decorated in rose and white balloons, and baskets of fresh flowers dotted every table. The caterers had served dinner, and now it was time for everyone to enjoy the party celebrating Gina and Nick's marriage.

Everything was changing so quickly. Just a few short months ago all of the Santini women had been sharing the family house. Now, it would be just Mama, Angela and Jeremy.

Her sisters were now officially halves of couples.

Marie and Davis.

Gina and Nick.

Angela and…she took a sip of champagne and turned away from the happy couple. No point in torturing herself, was there? Besides, it wasn't as if she *wanted* a husband. Not again. She just didn't want to end up a lonely old woman talking to cats and bothering her only son about bringing the grandchildren by more often.

Oh yeah, she thought grimly. Have some more champagne, it's really helping your attitude.

"So," Sam said, drawing her attention back to him, "what do you say to a dance with a lonely Marine?"

Lonely? She had a feeling Sam Paretti had never had a lonely day in his life.

"Sure," she said, "I—"

"Sorry, Marine," a deep voice said from behind Angela, "she's promised this one to me."

Angela's breath caught in her throat, and her stomach flip-flopped wildly.

"Is that right?" Sam asked, looking down at Angela.

"Uh," she cleared her throat, swallowed hard and said, "do you mind?"

The two men stared at each other for a long moment before Sam finally nodded. "I'll see you later, Angela."

"Thanks," she said as he turned and moved off into the crowd, leaving her alone with the man she'd been catching glimpses of all day.

"I've been looking for you," he said in a throaty whisper that tingled along her spine.

A quick spurt of excitement sizzled through her bloodstream as she turned around to face Dan.

They'd both been so busy doing wedding party things, they hadn't spoken since last night's interrupted dance. Well, they'd done more than just spoken, in Angela's dreams, but since he didn't know about that, it probably didn't count.

"Was I that hard to find?" she asked.

"Not for me," he said, leaning one hand on the wall above her head and bending closer. "I used to be Recon. Reconnaissance. The guys who go in, get what needs getting and get out."

He leaned in even closer, and Angela swore she could feel the warm brush of his breath against her cheek. Or maybe that was just her own heated blood flushing her face.

"You should know, I've been warned about you," Angela said as she looked up into the green eyes that had haunted her dreams all last night.

"Me?" Dan answered with that slow, crooked smile that was guaranteed to breach any defenses. "I'm harmless, lady."

Oh yeah, she believed that. And chocolate had no calories when eaten at midnight. Ha! She took another sip of champagne and silently reminded herself that she was on a mission here. She didn't want harmless. She wanted dangerous.

If just for tonight.

Actually, Gina's warning the night before had been the deciding factor in this. Knowing that Dan was interested in nothing more than a one-night stand made it all so easy. She could have one night of magic after far too long a dry spell, and there wouldn't be a single string attached. Well, except for the guilt strings she was already experiencing. Honestly, you wouldn't think it would be so hard for a twenty-eight-year-old widow to seduce a man. Another swallow of champagne followed the last, and a part of her brain reminded her that she wanted to be loose, not unconscious. But heck, who could blame her for trying a little liquid courage? It wasn't as if she did this every day.

"Harmless, huh?" she asked, giving him a smile she hoped was sexy. It had been so long, she couldn't be sure. "That's not what I hear."

"Who's been talking?"

Oh, brother, that smile of his should be classified as a lethal weapon. It did amazing things to a woman's equilibrium.

"Who hasn't?" she quipped.

"And do you always believe what you hear?" he asked, letting his gaze slide across her body with a slow, deliberately casual thoroughness.

Boy, he was better than she'd given him credit for. Her skin felt tight, and parts of her body she'd thought atrophied were galloping back to life. This was moving so fast she could hardly keep up. Taking a moment to calm down a bit, she looked around the room...actually, she looked anywhere but into those green eyes.

Angela studied the faces surrounding her, both familiar and strange. Dozens of Marines were sprinkled through the crowd, and she had to admit there was something about a man in a Dress-Blue uniform. It was an unfair advantage, really. No red-blooded woman, especially one who'd been living a celibate life for more than three years, could resist.

And the simple truth was, Angela didn't want to resist. She'd made up her mind what she was going to do the minute her sister Gina had told her that Dan was known on base as the king of the one-night stands. And she wasn't going to back out now.

"Want to try to finish our dance?" Dan asked, breaking into the thoughts swirling ceaselessly through her mind.

She inhaled and swiveled her head to look at him.

"For starters," she said bravely, and watched as desire flickered in the depths of his eyes. She half turned to set her champagne glass on the closest table, then he took her hand and led her through the crowd. Angela's gaze fixed on his broad back, narrow hips and long legs. A curl of anticipation unwound inside her, and her mouth went dry.

Ever since the night before, Angela hadn't been able to stop thinking about him. Sure, he was tall, dark and gorgeous. So were most of the other guys in the room. But there was something about First Sergeant Mahoney that made her blood boil and her usually cautious nature want to fly out the window.

And just for tonight, she was going to let it.

As they came to the middle of the dance floor, the music changed, shifting from a fast-paced, rock and roll number to an old Frank Sinatra standard. The voice of Ol' Blue Eyes swept into the room and was welcomed like an old friend. If she hadn't known better, she would have sworn Dan had planned it this way.

Dan pulled her into his arms and pressed her body to his. Her mouth went dry, and her head swam. She wasn't sure if it was the four or five glasses of champagne or the heady sensation of being held by a man again that was making her feel almost dizzy. And she didn't care. It was enough to be feeling again. To be experiencing that swift, sure punch of desire. The lick of flames at her center. The pooling warmth that threatened to collapse her knees and rob her of breath.

His right hand dropped to the curve of her behind as he eased her around the crowded dance floor. Subtly he pulled her tight against him. Hard and strong, his body pressed into hers, letting her know what she was doing to him. A rush of confidence filled her. She could still attract a man. Apparently the past three years of being a mom and a widow hadn't robbed her of her abilities to be a woman.

On his shoulder her left hand clutched at the fabric of his uniform. She leaned her head back to look up at him and struggled to continue breathing as he kept her pressed tightly to him.

"I sure hope I'm reading you right," Dan said, staring down at the woman he wanted more than his next breath.

She swallowed hard, then smoothed her left hand across his shoulders and down his back. "Trust me on this. If you weren't reading me right, you'd have known by now."

"Fair enough," he said, nodding, "but just to be safe, I'll say it plain. A simple no will end this. Now."

She stared at him, and he saw his own reflection in the soft-brown of her eyes. "And what does a yes get me?"

Dan's body tightened even further which he would have thought impossible a minute or two ago. Damn. He hadn't been expecting this. Stand up at his friend's wedding and end up sleeping with the friend's new sister-in-law?

"Lady," he said on a soft exhale of breath, "a yes will get you any darn thing you want."

She gave him a slow smile that set a match to the dynamite stacked inside him.

"That covers a lot of territory, First Sergeant."

"Yes ma'am," he promised, his brain filling with images of the night to come, "it surely does."

"Good," she said, and moved even closer to him, taking what little of his breath was left. "Then it's a date? After the bride and groom leave?"

"If I can wait that long," he said.

"It'll be worth the wait," she assured him, and stepped out of his arms as the song ended.

"Damn straight," he said tightly. He watched her as she moved back through the crowd, headed toward her sister. Her shoulder-length, dark-brown hair curved under at the ends and swung gently with each step she took. She wore a dark-pink bridesmaid's dress with a high collar, long sleeves and a full skirt that fell to her feet and brushed the floor in a soft, swishing sound as she moved. And that dress looked so damn good on her, he wondered if there was any way to convince Nick and Gina to take off on their honeymoon *now*.

"You're sure, honey?" Maryann Santini asked for the fiftieth time in the last ten minutes. "It just doesn't seem fair, all of us leaving you at the same time. I mean, Nick and Gina of course deserve their honeymoon, but it doesn't seem right for me to take off on a cruise right now."

"You and Margaret have been planning this for weeks," Angela reminded her mother patiently.

"I know, but now Jeremy's going to be gone, and even Marie and Davis are leaving town for a week."

Angela smiled at the thought of her eight-year-old son, but as much as she loved him, she was glad he'd asked to spend the weekend with his best friend. Especially now. With the plans she had for later tonight, home was no place for her son tonight.

"I'll be fine, Mama," she said, giving her mother a quick hug. "I'm a big girl, remember? I don't need a baby-sitter for heaven's sake. I'm actually looking forward to spending some time alone." Not completely alone, of course, but her mother didn't have to know *that*.

"All right, then," the older woman said, obviously still not convinced. "I'll only be gone ten days, and…"

The rest of her mother's words drifted into a stream of sound as Angela watched the last of the wedding guests filter out of the hall. The past two hours had crawled by. All she'd been able to think about was being alone with Dan Mahoney. It had been so long. So long since she'd been held, kissed, *touched*. Her body burned with an intensity she'd never known before. Every square inch of her skin seemed alive with sensation, as if she could almost feel his hands on her already.

"Are you listening to me?" her mother asked, laying one hand on Angela's forearm.

She jumped slightly, then tried to laugh it off. "I'm sorry, I must be tired."

"Actually your eyes look a little feverish," Mama said, frowning. "Are you sure you're feeling all right?"

Oh, she was feverish all right, but it was nothing aspirin could cure.

"I'm fine, Mama," she said, looking past her mother to the car pulling up opposite the doorway.

"Look, there's Margaret now. You'd better hurry or you'll miss your plane."

"All right then," Mama said, giving into the excitement of her first cruise. "You take care and make sure you lock the house and—"

"For heaven's sake, Mama," she said, impatience stampeding through her, "go."

"Okay, I'm going." Shaking her head, she hurried to her friend's car, opened the door and got in. Then with a wave of her hand and a honk of the horn, she was off.

Angela pulled in a deep breath and blew it out again. Alone. Finally alone. Jeremy had gone home with his friend Mike, the caterers would clean up the mess in the hall, Mama was taken care of. And that meant that for the first time in too long, Angela Santini Jackson, mother, daughter, sister, widow, could be, for tonight, anyway, simply Angela.

She headed for the parking lot on suddenly shaky legs. Her stomach spun, her mind raced as she asked herself if she was doing the right thing. This was so not her.

She just wasn't the one-night stand kind of woman.

Rounding the edge of the old brick building, she dug in her purse for her keys, and when she looked up, she saw Dan Mahoney, spotlit in the soft yellow glow of a parking lot lamp, leaning negligently against the hood of his car. Arms folded over his chest, feet crossed at the ankles, he stared at her from across the lot, and even at a distance Angela felt the power, the hunger in his gaze.

Her heartbeat quickened, and the parts of her body struggling back to life throbbed and hummed with an electrical pulse. She paused only briefly, then started toward him. Her heels tapped loudly against the asphalt and kept time with the pounding of her heart.

Her car was parked just a few spaces away from his. She stopped at the driver's side door, unlocked it and then looked at him.

He straightened up, moved over to her car and leaned both forearms on the roof. "So, Angela," he said softly, his voice whispering along her spine, "do we still have a date?"

She closed her eyes briefly, then looked at him again. If she said no, he'd leave, no harm done. There it is, she told herself. One last chance. One final opportunity to back out. To forget about the craziness of what she'd been planning and go back to her house alone.

She could pack away the box of condoms she'd purchased the night before and slide into her empty bed. She could dream her dreams and do without the soft slide of this man's hands on her skin.

Instead of feeling a man's arms around her, she could sit in the darkness and regret not having had the courage to take what she wanted. To, for once, put her own needs ahead of everyone else's.

The chilly, damp air swirled around her, and in

the soft tendrils of fog blowing in off the ocean, he looked almost otherworldly. As if he was only the dream image of a man. But she knew he was all too real, and that's exactly what she needed. What she wanted.

There would be no backing out.

Not tonight.

Swallowing hard, she said only, "I haven't changed my mind."

He nodded. "Me, neither."

Oh, my. The flash of desire glinted in his eyes and set off sparks deep within her. Her heart galloped, and she sucked in a gulp of air before opening the car door with a shaky hand. Then she looked directly into those amazing eyes of his and said, "You can follow me to my house."

He gave her a slow smile and nodded. "I'll be right behind you."

Three

Damn. He felt as keyed up as some randy teenager in the back seat of his father's Buick. Dan kept his gaze locked on Angela's taillights as she drove along the narrow streets toward her home. She made a left, turning onto a residential block that even in the darkness looked quiet and cozy. A *Leave It to Beaver* kind of neighborhood that ordinarily would have set off his internal radar and had him running in the opposite direction.

But not tonight.

Tonight there was nowhere else he'd rather be. Angela Jackson had dogged his mind and haunted his every thought since the moment he'd met her, and now he had to have her. If she'd sent him away, he would have had to crawl. His body was so eager for the joining that a *no* from her might have killed him.

Expectation whispered inside him and his body, already hard and ready, tensed further as she signaled a left turn into a driveway.

He glanced at the California bungalow-style house as he passed it. Then, making a U-turn in the middle of the block, he came back around and parked at the curb. Shutting off the engine, he took a moment to listen to the profound stillness. Slowly he swiveled his head to watch her climb out of her car.

Silhouetted against the backdrop of the porch light, he couldn't see her face, but he read her tension in every line of her body. Her tall, slim figure swayed a bit, and her floor-length skirt rippled around her.

Grabbing his keys, he got out of the car, locked it and shut the door with a solid thump that seemed to echo off the silent houses staring at him with dark windowpane eyes. Walking around the back of his car, he headed toward her. She didn't move, simply stood there, waiting for him.

His heart thundered in his chest, and when he came close enough to read her expression, even that beat accelerated. Desire, need, hunger, all shone in her eyes, feeding the emotions nearly strangling him.

He reached out and laid one hand on her forearm.

She shivered. Whether from eagerness or hesitation, he couldn't be sure. To satisfy the gentleman still crouched at the feet of the beast within, he forced himself to say softly, "Angela, if you don't want this, just say so."

She laughed shortly and tipped her head back to look up at him. "Want it?" she repeated, her voice thick and husky. "Dan, I want it so much it scares me."

That's all he needed to know. Turning her around, he led her toward the house and the brightly lit porch. They took the steps together, already moving as one, setting an unconscious rhythm. She fumbled with the keys, dropped them and Dan bent down to scoop them up.

"That one," she said.

He nodded, jammed it home and turned it. The lock snicked open, he turned the knob and ushered her inside. He stepped in right behind her, closed and locked the door, then turned to look at her.

Their gazes locked.

A heartbeat passed, then another.

Angela dropped her purse.

He let the keys clatter to the hardwood floor.

Then she was in his arms. He didn't know how she got there. He didn't remember moving toward her. He didn't know or care how they'd come together. He only knew that he couldn't seem to hold her close enough.

Taking her mouth, he plundered her, parting her

lips with his tongue, sweeping past any defenses she might have raised if she'd had time to think. He claimed her mouth fiercely, thoroughly. Again and again, his tongue mated with hers, twisting, twining, exploring and tasting. He sought her treasures, her secrets, and once he found them, searched for more. His hands moved up and down her back, over the curve of her behind where his fingers grabbed hold and squeezed, pulling her tightly to him.

Pressing her body to the straining, hard arousal that had tortured him all night brought a wave of pleasure so deep and rich it staggered him. He wanted more. He wanted it all.

Shifting his hands to the front of her dress, he slid them up, up past the swell of her breasts, to the wide collar that dipped so enticingly across her shoulders. He skimmed his fingertips across her skin and smiled to himself when she trembled in his grasp.

He tore his mouth from hers, and while she struggled to draw air into heaving lungs, he bent his head to kiss the curve of her neck. To taste the warmth of her skin, to tantalize her as she did him.

"Oh, my," she said on a short sigh, and tipped her head to one side, "that feels so—"

"Good," he finished for her.

"Beyond good," she assured him and leaned into him, pressing her breasts against his chest.

"I want to feel you," he said, letting his hands slide to the zipper at the back of her dress.

"Oh, yeah," she muttered, "that'd be good."

He smiled and tugged at the zipper, letting his fingertips trail along the line of exposed flesh as he went.

She shivered, and he groaned. She wasn't wearing a bra, and that fact fed the fires. Nothing stood between him and the feel of her breasts in his palms. The zipper went down, down, to just above the curve of her butt. Smooth skin called out for his touch and he obliged. Running his palms up and down her back, he worked the dress off and let it drop to a pool at her feet.

Angela stepped out of the fabric and kicked it aside.

The chill air in the room crawled over her body, and she hardly felt it. Her blood was boiling, and that was enough to keep her warm. She watched him watch her, and for the first time in years, worried about the lacy pattern of stretch marks across her not-entirely flat belly.

She wasn't exactly a cover model, after all. But when he lifted his hands and cupped her breasts, she stopped thinking. Who could care about stretch marks when his thumbs were stroking her already-pebbled nipples?

Angela rocked on her heels and closed her eyes. Sensation after sensation poured through her. From the top of her head to the tips of her toes, she was awash in the glory of *feeling*. It had been so long, so terribly long since her body had known the touch of a man.

She opened her eyes again and looked up into his heated gaze. Apparently, the same hunger tearing through her had a grip on him, too. Boldly, she reached up and fumbled with the brass buttons on his uniform tunic. Licking her lips, breathing hard, she worked at them until the Dress-Blue jacket was unbuttoned, unbelted, hanging open. She laid the flat of her hands against his white T-shirt-covered chest and felt the slam of his heartbeat against her palm.

Then he growled…actually *growled*…and yanked her to him. In seconds the rest of their clothes were gone, tossed aside, and she was held flush against his warm, naked, outrageously muscled body.

His hands swept up and down her back, then up and around to caress her breasts again. Every square inch of her body was electrified. Every nerve pushed to its breaking point. Desperate need coiled within her, building, growing, blossoming until she thought she might be consumed by it—and still she wanted more.

Dropping to the floor, he cushioned her head with his forearm and let his right hand slide down her length to the apex of her thighs. She held her breath, arched her back and lifted her hips in anticipation. His fingers dipped into her warmth, and her body exploded.

"Dan!" she cried, and clutched at him as a wild rush of tremors coursed through her. One after the other, tumbling into each other, never giving her a chance to catch her breath, the tiny explosions went on and on.

He held her tightly as the unexpectedly fierce climax claimed her. She rocked her hips against his hand, buried her face in the crook of his neck and rode the wave of sensation that carried her into a place she hardly remembered.

And when it was finally over and the last tremor shivered through her, she looked up at him. Good heavens, they'd hardly begun and she'd already finished. How mortifying was that? In a ragged voice she said, "It's been a long time. I'm sorry that happened so quickly."

He shook his head and smiled before leaning down to brush a kiss across her mouth. "Don't be sorry. I'm not."

Then he reached behind him for his trousers and fumbled one-handed for the pocket. Pulling out a foil-wrapped condom, he looked down at her. "I could use a little help with this, since I've only got the one free hand."

Keeping her gaze locked with his, she reached for it, tore it open, then slowly sheathed him. His eyes closed at her touch, and he moved closer. Angela wrapped her fingers around him, caressing him with smooth determined strokes. He arched into her and in seconds, her breath was coming fast, need coiled again inside her and she shifted into him, urging him to cover her. To fill her.

"Enough!" he muttered thickly, suddenly and moved to position himself between her thighs. Angela stared up at him as his fingers toyed with her tender flesh, smoothing, touching, exploring. She twisted and writhed in his grasp, giving herself up to the amazing things happening to her. In the glow of the foyer light, she watched his eyes darken and narrow with want and need, and she planted her feet firmly on the smooth wood floor and lifted her hips to welcome his first hard thrust.

She gasped at the intrusion, and a moment later felt her body adjust to his presence. Again and again he moved within her, setting a wild, fierce rhythm that she rushed to meet. She lifted her legs to lock them around his hips, pulling him tighter against her and deeper within her. Each time he withdrew, she wanted to moan the loss of him, and each time he rejoined their bodies, she wanted to shout at the glorious rightness of it.

He leaned over her, bracing his weight on his palms. Locking his gaze with hers, he set a soul-shattering pace that ended in a climax so powerful, so incredible, all Angela could do was hold on and hope she survived long enough to enjoy the afterglow.

And when she heard him groan tightly, she wrapped her arms around him and cushioned his fall.

Minutes…or maybe hours…flew by before either of them had the strength to move. Dan finally shifted to one side of her, pulling her with him, drawing her head onto his shoulder.

"That was," she said, and heard the hollowness in her own voice, "amazing."

He chuckled, and the sound rumbled through his chest. "*Amazing* is a pretty good word for it," he admitted, letting his hand slide up and down her arm.

"Well," she said, still enjoying the ripples of satisfaction trembling through her body. "I guess we could get up off the floor, huh?"

"What's the hurry?"

She tipped her head back on his shoulder and looked into hungry green eyes. "Hurry?" she whispered, then cleared her throat and tried again. "No hurry, but…well, we are finished and—"

"Finished?" he asked with a shake of his head, "We're just getting started."

"We are?" Oh, Lord, her heart was sure to pound right out of her chest any minute.

"Oh, yeah," Dan said, and shifted slightly to raise up on one arm. Trailing his fingertips along her body, from breast to hip, he smiled at the row of goose bumps that danced in his wake. "This time we take it slow."

''This time?'' she repeated. Heck, she hadn't recovered from the first time yet. Or the second mindnumbing climax. She had just spontaneously combusted all over her mother's shining wood floor.

Oh, she would never dust in here in peace again.

''This time,'' he said again, and rolled her onto her stomach before she could argue with him.

The cool wood planks beneath her lent another erotic touch to the moment. Spread-eagled on the foyer floor was not an image she'd ever had of herself. Yet here she lay, naked and eager for round two.

Then she felt his mouth at the base of her spine. His lips and tongue moved on her flesh and Angela shivered, clenching and unclenching her fists on nothingness, futilely looking for something to hold on to.

He spoke, and his breath brushed against her skin. ''I'm going to start at your spine, Angel,'' he said. ''Because your spine is connected directly to your brain. And this time I'm going to make love to your mind as well as your body.''

Oh, my, she thought and let her eyes close.

He kissed her, running his lips and tongue along the column of her spine, tasting her, learning every curve, every line. He'd wanted her so badly right from the start and now that he'd had her, enjoyed her, felt her body cradling his, it wasn't enough. He wanted even more of her, and this was a first for him.

Usually, when that initial rush of desire had been sated, he was content, and ready to move on. He didn't want commitment. Relationships. Now, though, with this woman, all Dan could think of was *more*. More of her. More of *them*.

His hands drifted over her flesh, and when she stirred beneath him, he knew her body, too, was flickering back into life. Back into need. At the nape of her neck, he nibbled at her skin until rows of goose bumps dotted her back and shoulders. She writhed beneath him, but he didn't ease her discomfort, instead, he stoked it. With touch after touch, kiss after kiss, he fed the fires engulfing them both and hoped they'd be consumed by them.

And when touching her wasn't enough any more, he turned her over, scooped her into his arms and muttered, "Bedroom?"

"Upstairs," she whispered, locking her arms around his neck and laying her head on his chest. "Hurry."

"You bet," he said, and took the stairs two at a time.

"Second door."

"Right." He went up to it, stepped into a cool, mint-green room with a lacy cover on the bed and more lace covering the windows, where moonlight tried to peek through the patterns of frothy fabric.

Walking directly to the bed, he reached down with one hand and swept the coverlet down to the foot of the mattress. Then he laid Angela down atop the pale-green sheets and stretched out beside her. Dipping his head to her breasts, he took first one nipple and then the next into his mouth.

Her hands fisted in his hair as she held him tightly to her. His tongue stroked the pebbly surface of her nipples, and he tasted them both until he'd had his fill. Until she was moving and moaning beneath him. And then he began again.

"Dan..." she whispered, arching into him, turning toward him. "I need you. Now."

"Slow this time, Angel. Slow for both of us." Though it killed him to maintain control, he wanted to make this last. To make this joining even more complete than the first.

She chuckled harshly and shook her head. "I don't think I can stand slow."

He smiled against her breast and let one hand slide down along her body to the warm heart of her.

She gasped as he cupped her and lifted her hips into his touch.

"Oh, now I *know* I can't wait much longer."

"It gets better," he assured her.

"Impossible," she murmured, twisting her hips into his touch.

"Trust me," he said and shifted, moving down along her body, trailing damp kisses and silent promises as he went.

He glanced up at her and saw her hands pulling at the fine linen sheets, and holding them tightly.

And he smiled to himself, enjoying the fact that he could bring her to this point again so soon after that mind-numbing pleasure they'd shared only moments ago.

"Dan...Dan," his name came on a gasp of sound as her breath quickened. She licked dry lips and tossed her head from side to side on the pillow as she tried to find the release only he could give her.

He moved to take a place between her thighs and, kneeling, lifted her behind off the bed in a gentle, firm grip. His fingers kneaded the tender flesh as he lifted her higher and bent his head to taste her.

Angela gasped aloud and looked at him as his mouth took her places she hadn't dreamed existed. No man *ever* had done this to her before. And she wouldn't have believed that she would not only allow it, but luxuriate in the sensations she was feeling.

He'd been right. He'd claimed not only her body but her mind this time. Her brain spinning, her heartbeat thundering in her ears, she struggled to hold on to what was left of her sanity as another part of her raced toward the release she knew was awaiting her.

His mouth and tongue tortured her with sweet deliberation. His breath dusted across tender flesh as he pushed her higher, higher until she felt as though the air was too thin to breathe. And just when she thought she couldn't bear the suspense any longer, his intimate kiss sent her spiraling over the edge of sanity into a soft oblivion.

And a moment later Dan's body entered hers, and in a few quick, hard thrusts, he found a sense of completion he'd never known before.

As he collapsed atop her, he realized that here, in the quiet rooms of a well-tended home, he'd made her his and fallen into a tender trap he'd never seen coming.

Four

She took a short nap—or passed out, she wasn't really sure which. But when she woke, the first thing Angela heard was her own stomach growling. She'd been so stressed, so focused on her seduction of Dan Mahoney, she'd hardly eaten a thing all day.

"Hungry, huh?" he asked, turning his head on the pillow to look at her.

She slapped one hand atop her abdomen as though with a little pressure from the outside, she might stop all the grumbling on the inside. When it continued, she gave him a half smile. "Apparently, yes."

"Me, too. So," he suggested, pushing himself up and off the bed, "let's raid your kitchen."

Not a bad idea, she thought. If she could move. Muscles she hadn't used in years ached with a tenderness that was both tiring and exhilarating. As she looked up at him, he seemed to sense what she was feeling.

Giving her a half grin, he stretched out one hand to her and said, "C'mon, I'll help you up."

"Uh…" Okay, sharing a tremendously satisfying sexual experience was one thing. Strolling around naked was something else again. "Could you hand me my robe first?" she asked. "It's there on the chair behind you."

He glanced at it, then shook his head. "Feeling shy all of a sudden?"

Angela inhaled sharply. "Not *shy,* just…" Ridiculous, she told herself. The man had spent the past hour exploring her entire body, up close and personal. A little late to try to cover it up now.

"Come on, Angel," he said, grabbing her hand and pulling her from the bed.

Angel. No one had shortened her name like that since she was a child. She was either Angela or Mom or, rarely, Angie. But not Angel. Looking into those killer-green eyes of his, she let him pull her to her feet. When she stood in front of him, she had to tilt her head back to keep meeting his eyes. Which was way safer than looking anywhere else.

"No reason to be bashful. There's no one here but you and me," he said, and lifted one hand to cup her right breast.

Her knees shook. She locked them.

His thumb stroked her nipple.

Angela trembled.

And the shiver seemed to transfer directly into him. He blew out a breath, let his hand drop to his side, then bent down and planted a quick, hard kiss on her mouth. She was still licking the taste of him off her lips when he said gruffly, "Snack. Keep our strength up."

"Strength," she murmured, her voice shaking. "Need strength. A good thing."

"Oh, yeah," he muttered thickly.

"Mmm…" She stumbled after him as he tugged her from the room, into the hallway and down the stairs.

Their bare feet whispered against the carpet runner on the old staircase. Shadows reached out for them, cloaking them in a dimly lit world where tomorrows and yesterdays didn't matter. All that existed was the present. In all its glory.

The stove light cast a weird, pale glow across the kitchen, and neither of them hit the overhead light switch. He headed for the fridge, while Angela went to the old-fashioned wooden bread box on the counter.

"Turkey?" he asked, lifting his head to glance at her.

"Sounds good," she said, getting out bread and plates and a couple of knives.

He carried the sandwich fixings and a couple of

bottles of water to where she stood and set them down.

"Didn't get much to eat at the wedding," she said, more to break the silence than any other reason. Of course she wasn't about to admit that *he* was the reason she hadn't been able to choke down any food. She'd been able to think of nothing but seducing the man now standing naked next to her.

Oh, heavens. She was standing in her mother's kitchen, naked. Her hands shook as she reached for the mustard.

"Me, neither," he admitted, glancing at her. "I was too busy watching you."

Oh, my.

"But everything looked good," he said.

Angela smiled, remembering the long tables groaning under the weight of the food collected for the reception. "It did, didn't it?" Then with pride coloring her tone, she added, "Gina set it all up, you know."

"She cooked all that food?"

Angela chuckled at the astonishment in his voice. Gina hadn't had the time to do everything, but if she'd had time, there wasn't a doubt in Angela's mind that her little sister could have. "No. She did all the decorating and arranged for the different caterers and even sweet-talked a friend of Mama's into making a mountain of lasagna."

"Mmm," he muttered. "Now that sounds good right about now, doesn't it?"

It did indeed, but...

"Sorry," she said as she picked up her sandwich. "You'll have to settle for turkey."

He looked at her as she took a bite and said, "I like the atmosphere here better."

Now how did he expect her to be able to swallow if he continued to close up her throat with comments like that? She took a swig of water and turned toward the table. Sitting down, she hissed in a breath as the cold wooden chair made contact with her bare backside.

"Cold?" he asked, sitting next to her.

"I've never really tried sitting here naked before."

"Well now," he said with a smile. "That's a shame. Naked looks good on you."

There went her throat again.

Clearing her throat, she tried for conversation. Anything to keep her mind from fixating on the fact that she was sitting naked beside a man she'd just made wild, passionate love with.

"So, how long have you known Nick?" There. Bringing up her sister and brand-new brother-in-law ought to be enough to keep her hormones in check.

"A couple of years," he said, and idly stroked his fingertips along her upper thigh.

Angela breathed deeply, evenly. Her hormones were on hyperdrive and apparently, there was no stopping them.

"He seems nice," she said.

"He's a good guy."

Scintillating conversation, Angela. Way to go. She chewed another bit of turkey as her mind twisted and tumbled, searching for something to say. Something to explain to him how she happened to be here with him. Naked.

Strange how the word *naked* kept coming to mind.

"You know," she said, shifting slightly to move her leg out from under his hand, "I want you to understand that this isn't something I usually do."

"Eat turkey sandwiches in the middle of the night?" he asked, smiling.

"No," she said pointedly. "Eat turkey sandwiches *with a naked man* in the middle of the night."

"Ahh…" He nodded, and one dark eyebrow lifted into an arch.

"I mean…" What did she mean, anyway? She didn't owe him an explanation, did she? Wasn't it enough that they were two grown people who could spend one unencumbered night together? Nope, apparently not.

"What I mean is," she said, setting her sandwich down and half turning toward him, "I'm not the kind of woman who usually—"

"Sleeps with a guy she hardly knows?" Dan finished for her.

"Yeah," she said, although the way he'd just

described it made her feel a little sleazy. Good Lord, what had she been thinking?

"I know that," he said, and his voice was deep and low and intimate.

"You do?"

"Yeah, I do." Dan studied her in the pale, soft light and found her to be even more gorgeous than she'd looked to him the first time he'd laid eyes on her.

Her shoulder-length hair was ruffled and stood out around her head like a dark halo. Her lips were soft and full from his kisses, and her brown eyes looked as deep and wide as the night sky. A fresh, swift rush of desire pulsed through him as he let his gaze drift over her, from the long line of her throat to the swell of her breasts, to the rigid nipples that seemed to be beckoning his touch.

She was nothing like the sweet young things he usually dated, with their sometimes too-thin bodies and their aggressive, take-no-prisoners attitudes. But until tonight he'd always been happy, never thought of himself as missing something. For good reason, his game plan had always been to spend a pleasurable evening and then beat it. Get back to his house. Where he could be alone. He'd never been much for the cuddle-and-chat side of the "afterglow."

But with Angela…this was a woman. In every sense of the word. Her body was rounded and generous and lush and showed the faint traces of having borne a child. And Dan found that lacy pattern of old scars to be incredibly erotic. In fact everything about Angela Jackson was erotic. From the way she tossed her hair back out of her face to the way she licked her lips after taking a sip of water.

And it was all unconscious. It wasn't as though she was *trying* to be seductive. She simply was. And he'd known, from the moment he'd touched her tonight, that she hadn't been with anyone in a long time. She'd admitted as much herself right after her body had exploded with his first touch. Her shy eagerness, her soft sighs, all fed a fire inside him that even now was flickering back to life.

"Look, Angel," he said when she shifted again under his steady stare, "for whatever reason, we're here. Together. Tonight. Let's let it be enough for now, okay?"

She thought about it for a moment, then nodded. "Okay."

"Good," he said, and scooted close enough that he could run his fingers along her thigh again, and this time she didn't move away. He buried the smile inside and asked, "So what do you do? For a living, I mean?"

She shuddered, licked her lips and whispered, "I teach. Third grade."

Now he did smile. "I don't remember having teachers as pretty as you when I was a kid."

She swallowed heavily. "Thanks."

"Of course," he went on, "I was taught by nuns."

She laughed. "You, too?"

"Catholic school survivor," he said, lifting one hand as if swearing to an oath.

"How many years?" she asked, still grinning.

"Eight."

"Hah!" she said triumphantly. "I did twelve years hard time."

"You win," he said. "I switched to a public high school."

Angela shook her head. "Lucky you. The Santini girls did bobby sox and uniforms right up through high school graduation."

"You're a braver soul than I am," he conceded. "And I'm a professional soldier."

"Soldiers!" Angela laughed. "I've known nuns who could make mincemeat out of a Navy SEAL team."

"Me, too," he said on a chuckle. "In fact, Sister Alphonsus still shows up in my nightmares on occasion." Shaking his head, he mused, "I've been in combat, and let me tell you, I've never been as scared as I was in that woman's algebra class."

Another silence descended, but this one was easier, more friendly somehow.

"Do you have any brothers and sisters?" Angela asked a few minutes later.

"One sister," he said, smiling at the thought of

Melissa. "She's married to a football coach. They've got three girls. Live in Wyoming."

"And your parents?"

"Alive and well, retired to Florida a few years back."

She nodded.

"Your dad?" he asked.

Angela gave him a small smile. "He died about two years ago."

Nodding, he thought he maybe shouldn't ask this, but he did want to know. "And your husband?"

She stiffened slightly under his touch, and he knew his instincts had been right. He never should have brought the man up.

"He died three years ago."

"I'm sorry."

"Thank you," she said, pushing what was left of her sandwich to the center of the table. "But it was a long time ago."

"I'm sorry for mentioning him."

"Don't be. I'm fine."

She wasn't. He could see the tension in the lift of her chin and in the rigid set of her shoulders. But he could do something about that. He could make her forget whatever bad memories were now clouding her eyes and wrinkling her brow.

Standing up, he drew her to her feet, too.

"You know," she said, "it's awfully late and—"

He kissed her. Not giving her a chance to ask

him to leave. Not giving her a chance to push what they'd shared under a mental rug. Not giving her a chance to close up and shut him out.

His mouth moved on hers for a few seconds before he felt her begin to give as well as take. Her surrender came sweet and soft. And as their mouths mated, she moved in close to him, molding her breasts to his chest, aligning her body with his until he was hard and ready and nearly desperate with want.

Her hands stroked up and down his back, her fingertips playing with the line of his spine, and he felt each touch like a tiny flame. Like dozens of struck match heads, eruptions of heat blistered his skin and seared his soul.

He held her tighter, closer, and still it wasn't enough. Breaking the kiss, he gasped in a breath and muttered, "Now."

She nodded frantically, sending her hair flying into her eyes, then swinging it back out of her way. "Yes," she said thickly, "now."

Her bedroom was too far away. The staircase leading to the second story might as well have been a hundred miles away. He couldn't wait. He needed her. More than he could ever remember wanting anyone or anything before.

Turning around, he grabbed her by the waist, lifted her and sat her down on the kitchen counter. Angela gasped at the cold shock of Formica against her skin. But after only a heartbeat of time, she wrapped her legs around his middle and drew him close.

Then sanity intruded with a white-hot stab of reality that shot across Dan's brain and stopped him flat. "We can't," he ground out. "Not here. Condoms are upstairs, damn it."

Angela pulled his head toward her and kissed him, long and slow and deep, then pulled her head back and shook her head. "It's taken care of," she said breathlessly. "As long as you're…"

"Healthy?" he asked.

"Yeah." She licked her lips, and he wanted to bite that tongue.

"I am."

"Thank heavens."

Blood pulsing through him, he still had to be sure. "So it's all right? Safe?"

"The Pill," she whispered, moving in to claim another kiss between her words. "On it for years."

"Thank heavens," he echoed, and gave her the kiss she'd been diving for as he entered her on a swift, hard thrust that stole both his breath and hers. She scooted forward on the counter, pulling him deeper within her body. His hands cupped her behind and held on, his fingers clenching tightly into her flesh.

Again and again he advanced and retreated into her tight warmth, the only sound in the house her moans and sighs. Her body cradled his in a soft fist. He took her and was taken. Gave and received. His mind blanked, and his body hummed. She held his face in her palms, parted her lips and took what was left of his breath for her own.

And when the heart-shattering climax claimed them both, she clutched at him as though he was the only stable point in her suddenly rocking universe.

He bent his head to hers and waited until his heartbeat had settled into a stable rhythm again. She cuddled into him, and his arms came tight around her. And a minute or two later, still locked within her body, Dan picked her up and carried her out of the kitchen, through the shadows and back up the stairs to her bedroom.

Then together they fell onto the mattress and into a dreamless void.

Five

Angela hardly recognized herself.

Was she the same woman who'd lived like a nun for the past three years? Was she the same woman who'd hardly been interested in her husband's clumsy attentions on those rare nights when he had noticed she was there? Was *this* the third-grade teacher? The chairman of the Carnival Committee? The sedate widow and mother of an eight-year-old boy?

Nope, she thought with a small grin as she stretched like a well-fed cat on the now-rumpled sheets of her bed. This was someone entirely different. This was a wild, sexy, apparently insatiable free spirit.

And damned if she hadn't enjoyed every minute of it.

Still, she told herself with a glance at the window opposite her bed, dawn was beginning to color the sky, and even Cinderella had been forced to leave the ball eventually.

She turned her head on the pillow to look at the man lying beside her. A quick, hot flash of something wicked shot through her, and again she was amazed at herself. She'd never suspected that she was such a sensual creature.

Sex had never been more than a mildly pleasant exercise in keeping her husband happy. Until, of course, she'd gone without the last three years. But she'd told herself it was the closeness she'd missed. The sensation of being held, of feeling that solid, heavy weight pressed down on top of her.

Angela had expected to enjoy herself with Dan. She simply hadn't expected to *enjoy* herself with Dan. It had been…magical.

But at that thought she told herself to get a grip. Cinderella and magic had nothing to do with her life. The night was over, and now it was back to reality.

Reaching out, she laid one hand on his cheek. "Time to wake up, Dan," she said softly, and smiled when his eyes opened instantly and looked directly into hers.

"What time is it?" he muttered, and rose onto one elbow.

"Almost six," she said and sat up, drawing the sheet with her, to hold across her naked breasts. Pointless to try to hide her body from him, since he'd already seen every square inch of it, but, there you go.

"Already?" he muttered.

"Yep," she said smiling, "and before you go, I'd just like to say...thanks. I haven't felt this good in years."

"Before I go?" he repeated, focusing on only one part of that sentence.

"Well, yes," she said, "it's morning."

"So?" One corner of his mouth tilted up, and she felt a small but significant tug at her insides.

"So," she went on, a little slower now, "our night together's over."

He glanced out the window at the pearly light just beginning to ease across the sky, then nodded and scrubbed one hand across his face. "I suppose it is," he said, then looked at her again. "Have you got any plans for this morning?"

"Plans?"

"Yeah," he said, giving her a full-blown smile that sent a rush of tingles right down to her toes. "You know, things to do?"

"No," she admitted, remembering that Jeremy was going to be at his friend's house for the whole weekend. "Actually, I have the house to myself for a couple of days."

"Then there's no rush?" he asked quietly.

"I guess not," she said, although being frisky and wanton came a lot easier in darkness than it did in the growing light of day.

"So," he was saying, "how about a shower and some coffee?"

Seemed reasonable, she told herself as he rolled out of bed and headed for the bathroom. Her gaze locked on his broad back, narrow hips and tight rear. Oh, my, she thought as the now-familiar rush of liquid fire poured into her veins.

He stopped at the open door leading into the bathroom, half turned, looked at her and held out one hand toward her. Smiling, he asked, "Save water, shower with a friend?"

Hey, she was as ecologically minded as the next person. Besides, with an invitation like that, what sane woman could refuse?

She scooted off the bed, and in the soft hush of dawn light, walked naked across the room, slipped her hand into his and mentally gave Cinderella one last dance at the ball.

Hot needles of water pelted them, and the steam rose up to creep across the top of the shower rod to fog the mirrors. Behind the cream-colored plastic curtain, Dan soaped up his hands and then caressed Angela's shoulders and back, smoothing his hands up and down her flesh with long, leisurely strokes.

He couldn't seem to get enough of her. Every time she sighed, the soft sound slipped inside him and rattled what was left of his control, his composure. He told himself it was simply sex. No more, no less than he'd found with other women at other times, but even Dan wasn't buying that one. This was more. How much more he didn't know. Didn't *want* to know.

"I've never done this before," she said, and her quiet words were almost swallowed by the rush of the water. "Taken a shower with a man, I mean."

"Not even with your husband?" he asked, wondering what kind of idiot she'd been married to.

She laughed shortly. "Lord, no," she said, and groaned a bit as his hands rubbed at her shoulders.

"Well then," he said, sliding his soapy hands down her back to the rounded curve of her behind. She trembled, and he smiled to himself. "I'm pleased to be the man to introduce you to it."

Her shoulder-length hair lay slick against her head and neck. He pulled her into his grasp, her back to his front, and let her lean heavily against him as he worked soap bubbles across her breasts and then down.

"Mmm," she murmured, "feels wonderful..."

She gasped aloud as his fingers entered her, working her body with the tender deliberation of a master musician. She slapped her right hand against the shower stall and opened her eyes wide as he continued. The fast, sliding motions of his fingers shot her toward a staggering ecstasy that had her yelling his name as her body bucked against his hand.

And when the last of the pulsing tremors had eased away, she groaned tightly and shook her head. "I'll never survive this...."

He grinned and held her up straight under the shower spray. As the water cascaded off her bent head, he said, "Angel, I'm a Marine. Trust me. I'll get you through it."

An hour or so later she walked him to his car, congratulating herself on the fact that she was able to walk at all. Her legs felt like overcooked spaghetti. She was tired, a little achy and, all in all, hadn't felt this good in years. Shoving her hands into the front pockets of her jeans, Angela strolled barefoot across the grass, still damp with dew. She tipped her head back to look up at the cloud-swept sky, then smiled to herself as she slanted her glance at the man beside her. In the early-morning light, Dan looked every bit as delicious in his Dress-Blue uniform as he had in the moonlight.

A quick skitter of something warm and silky rushed through her, and as she stopped at the edge of the yard, Angela tried to get a grip on her rapidly racing hormones.

He opened the driver's side door, glanced down the street at the wakening neighborhood, then leaned both arms on the hood of his car as he looked across it at her. "Last night was amazing."

Her stomach flip-flopped. *Amazing* was a good word for it, all right. And this morning hadn't been too shabby, either. "Yes, it was," she said when she could get her voice to work.

"You said you didn't have any plans for this weekend, right?" he asked.

"Yeah…"

He smiled, and Angela's toes curled. "Well," he said, "Then how about a movie tonight?"

Tonight? Her mind raced. She hadn't planned on this. She'd figured…no, *counted* on his reputation as a one-night stand kind of guy. And now he wanted to stretch their time together beyond what she'd been expecting?

"A date, you mean?" Angela asked, taking her hands from her pockets and wrapping her arms around her middle to ward off the early morning chill that was just beginning to seep into her bones.

"Why not?" he asked, turning up the wattage on that smile of his.

"Oh, I don't know if that's a good idea," she said, shaking her head. One-night stands didn't work if they suddenly became two, did they?

"It's just a movie," he said with a shrug.

She sighed and let her gaze drift from his to scan the sleepy street. Mrs. Johnson stepped off her front porch to snag the morning paper out of its customary spot in the shrubbery. Jamie Hill slammed his front door and took off on his morning jog. Francine Kramer began the morning ritual of calling to

her reluctant cat. The plaintive call "Fluffy...
Fluffy..." lifted into the still air, and Angela shook
her head.

Everything was the same, and yet she was so
different. She'd just spent a glorious, wild, completely satisfying evening with a man who was
practically a stranger. What would the neighbors
have to say about that? she wondered. And she had
no doubt at all that every one of the people who
had noticed Dan Mahoney leaving her house at the
crack of dawn would be talking about it.

Probably a good thing they didn't make you walk
around with a big red *A* on your shirt anymore. But
then *A* for *adulterer* didn't really fit in her case.
Maybe a big red *S* for *Sleaze bucket*...

"Angela?"

His voice brought her back and she looked at
him, staring into those green eyes of his. This is a
mistake, she told herself. A truly big mistake. And
even knowing that, she heard herself say, "Okay.
A movie." Then, realizing that she'd better let him
know right from the get-go that her brief, yet mem-
orable trip onto the wild side was now officially
over, she added, "But *just* a movie, right?"

"Sure," he said and slapped one hand onto the
roof of his car. "Just a movie. See you tonight."

"Tonight."

As he climbed in and fired up the engine, Angela
worried her bottom lip. Tonight. When it would be
dark again. And she would still be alone in the

house. Oh, man. This really wasn't a good idea at all. But then he stepped on the gas and his black Chevy Blazer pulled away from the curb and it was too late to call him back. Too late to change her mind.

Too late to chicken out.

Even if she'd wanted to.

It was one of those romantic comedies that usually left a woman smiling through her tears and a man staring blankly at the darkening screen, wondering what in the heck the big deal was. As the houselights came up and the audience slowly drifted toward the exit, Dan turned his head to look at the woman beside him.

She dabbed at her eyes with the corner of a paper napkin and smiled when she caught him watching her.

Shrugging, she said, "I always cry at happy endings."

And damned if he didn't find that touching. In the dim light, her eyes shimmered and shone and her wobbly smile tugged at his heart.

Oh, he was in some potentially serious trouble here.

He'd known it all day. He hardly remembered what he'd done at work. Somehow he'd put in his time on base, dealt with the everyday problems that seemed to crop up continually and still thought about little else but Angela.

This just wasn't normal. Not for him. Usually he could separate his work and his personal life. He'd never before run into a woman whose memory stayed with him long after they'd parted. And he'd never felt...hell, he didn't even know what he was feeling. All he was sure of was that he'd never experienced it before, and that worried him.

Yet still he hadn't been able to stay away. He couldn't risk feeling—and then failing.

And when she'd opened the front door to him a couple of hours ago, it had been all he could do to keep from holding her, kissing her. He sucked in a gulp of air and pushed that thought into a corner of his mind.

"Happy endings, huh?" he asked. "Love conquers all? Happily ever after?"

She tossed the napkin into the empty popcorn bucket and set it on the floor. "It makes for a good movie."

"But not real life?"

Angela smiled and shook her head. "I stopped waiting for a knight in shining armor to come riding to my rescue a *long* time ago."

Smart woman, he thought, yet at the same time noticed the flicker of disappointment in her eyes. And he couldn't help wondering why she didn't expect a happy ending for herself. Then he had to wonder why that fact bothered him.

Hell, if he had any sense at all, he would take her home and run back to base. He'd forget about this weekend and the woman with the soft-brown eyes and the lush curves. He would put Angela Jackson firmly in the past and leave her there. Because he didn't want to hurt her. And if he stayed...he would.

Shaking the thought off, he pushed himself to his feet, held out a hand toward her and, when she took it, pulled her up beside him. "Well, I'm no knight," he said, giving her a smile, "and you don't look like you need rescuing, but what do you say to letting a Marine buy you an ice cream cone?"

She ducked her head briefly, pulled her hand free of his, then looked up at him. "Look, Dan, it's not that I don't appreciate it, but—"

"I know," he cut in, "we said just a movie." He lifted one hand to brush back a long strand of her hair. "But it's just ice cream, Angel. I'll take you home right after."

She studied him for a long minute, then nodded. "All right."

"Good." Taking her hand again, he led her out of the row of seats, down the steps and around to the narrow aisle that led to the exits.

On the pier Angela walked beside him, enjoying his company almost as much as she enjoyed the chocolate-brownie ice cream cone. A spring night in California brought out the crowds. Though cool enough to warrant a light sweater, which she didn't have with her, since she hadn't planned on a walk on the pier, the weather was nice enough to draw the people already hungering for summer.

Yellow fog lights staggered down the length of the old wooden pier and threw pools of eerie light into the darkness. People, young and old, strolled up and down the length of the long wooden jetty, talking, laughing and dodging the in-line skaters who darted in and out of the crowd with the grace of ballet dancers. Couples walked hand in hand, oblivious to the other people around them, and groups of teenage girls chattered and giggled as they watched the boys pretend not to notice them.

The combined scents of ocean air, frying hamburgers and fish seemed familiar, almost cozy.

Moonlight and fog lights dazzled on the surface of the ocean, and long streamers of clouds trailed ghostly fingers across the sky. Angela shivered as a rush of cold, damp air swept along the pier, tugging at those it passed.

"Cold?" Dan asked, already stripping out of his dark-blue sweatshirt.

"A little," she admitted, and smiled at him when he laid his sweatshirt across her shoulders. "Thanks."

"The least a knight could do."

"Knight, huh?" she asked, and walked to one side of the pier, stepping around the cement benches to reach the rail. Leaning both elbows on the rough surface of the wooden railing, she asked, "That's what Marines are? Modern-day knights?"

He shrugged, took up a position beside her and thoughtfully studied his ice cream. "We are whatever's needed."

She shifted her gaze to the handful of wet-suit-clad surfers sitting on their boards in the darkness below. "Cowboys?"

"Sure."

"Pirates?"

He chuckled. "When we have to be."

"Heroes for all seasons, then, huh?" She glanced at him.

"Yep," he said with a smile and a nod. "Professional hero. That's me."

Strangely enough, she didn't have any problem at all with that description of him. Tall, strong, gentle yet passionate, he really was the prototypical Hollywood hero.

If she was looking for a hero. Which she wasn't.

He took a bite of his ice cream, and when he licked his lips, Angela sighed and looked away again for her own sake. Her gaze fell on a man and his son, night fishing a few feet away from them.

The boy was about Jeremy's age, and he was all but hopping from foot to foot in excitement. His father lowered a light over the side of the pier, explaining that the fish would swim up to the light to investigate it and then maybe take a bite of the bait they'd offer them.

She smiled to herself as she watched, thinking of

Jeremy and how much he would enjoy fishing off the pier.

"Cute kid," Dan said close to her ear.

"Yes," she said, not even turning to look at him.

"Your son, Jeremy, is about that age, right?"

"Yeah, about."

"He seems like a nice kid," Dan said, and she turned to look at him. "I mean, from what I saw of him at the rehearsal dinner and the wedding."

"Thanks," Angela said, and felt the rush of pride that always filled her at thoughts of her son. "I think so, too, but—"

"But…?"

She shook her head and glanced back at the father and son. "Sometimes I worry," she said softly. "You know, a boy his age needs a father and—"

"I didn't have one," Dan said quietly.

"Really?" she asked, shifting her gaze back to him. "What happened?" Then as soon as the question was out of her mouth, she tried to retract it. "No. Never mind. I'm sorry. It's none of my business."

He chuckled again and took another bite of his ice cream before saying, "Relax, Angel. Doesn't matter. It was a long time ago."

It was too dark to read his eyes, but his expression was casually blank, so maybe it didn't bother him to talk about it. "Then, if you don't mind…"

"My father left us," Dan said, letting his gaze slide out to the wide-open expanse of the sea. "I was about seven, I guess. After that, it was just Mom and us.''

He felt her gaze on him, and Dan made a point of shielding his emotions, his memories.

"So you didn't mind?" she asked, worry still plain in her voice. "You didn't miss having a father?"

No, he thought. What he'd minded was his mother mourning the man who'd left them. For years she'd searched the mailbox for a letter from the man who'd broken her heart. She'd waited, Dan knew, hoping her husband would come home. Hoping he would tell her he was sorry. That he'd made a mistake. But as the years passed, she'd finally come to accept what was, and she'd never missed the chance to tell her only son that it hadn't really been his father's fault. That all men were bastards. That even the best of them would end up hurting the ones they loved. And that he, Dan, would one day grow up to be just like his father.

He could still hear her telling him that he couldn't help it. It was just the way things were and that if he really wanted to be kind, he wouldn't make promises he'd only end up breaking.

"Dan?"

Angela's voice came from beside him and effectively closed the door on old memories. Putting a mental padlock on that door, he remembered what they'd been talking about, and quickly groped for a good answer. Taking a deep breath, he said,

"Sure, you miss having a dad. But you learn to live with it."

"I suppose," she said, but didn't sound convinced.

"Besides," he said, a bit more heartily than he felt, "Jeremy's got Nick for an uncle now. He'll do right by the kid."

"That's true, isn't it?" Angela asked, turning her head to watch the father and son talking and laughing together again. "My sisters' husbands can be the role models he needs."

"Why not?" Dan asked. "Two more professional heroes. Substitute dads don't come much better than that."

"Knights in khaki armor?"

"Ooh-rah," he said, and smiled down into those chocolate eyes.

Six

They strolled along the pier, and Angela marveled at how easy Dan was to talk to. He made her laugh at his stories about life in the Marines, and he asked questions about her life as though he were really interested. A heady experience, considering that even when her late husband Bill had been alive, he'd rarely asked her opinion on anything.

And in the three years since she was widowed, she'd come to appreciate the quiet of her own thoughts. She hadn't been interested in finding another man. She'd avoided the pitfalls of pity fix ups and blind dates. She'd ignored the friends who had told her to move on. To pick up her life and find someone new. Someone to love her as she deserved to be loved.

Because she just couldn't risk it. She couldn't risk making another mistake, because this time it wasn't just her heart on the chopping block…it was Jeremy's too.

And yet, here she was, taking a moonlight stroll with a man who stirred up far too many emotions.

"Let's go down," Dan said.

"What?" she asked, turning to look up at him.

"Down there. To the sand," he said, pointing to the nearly empty stretch of beach below them.

"I'm not exactly dressed for beachcombing," she said, and waved one hand at her pastel-blue skirt and matching heels.

He smiled at her. "Take 'em off."

"Excuse me?"

The smile broadened. "Your shoes, Angel. Just your shoes."

"Oh." Dumb, Angela, she told herself. Really dumb.

"I wouldn't expect you to strip on the beach until at least July," he went on, clearly enjoying her embarrassment. "Way too cool for it now."

"Gee, thanks," she said, shaking her head.

"So?" he asked. "What do you say?"

What *could* she say? No. More to the point, what did she *want* to say? "Sure. Why not?"

He took her hand and led her to the end of the pier, where a set of stairs wound down to the sand. At the bottom, he caught sight of the broken bits of glass lying in wait for the unwary and half turned to her. Before she could wonder what he was up to, he picked her up and marched across the sand.

"Hey, I'm capable of walking, you know."

"Yeah, I know," he said, looking down at her upturned face. "But this is more fun."

Fun? She wasn't exactly a ninety-eight-pound weakling. Okay, she wasn't a heavyweight, either, but still, he wasn't even winded as he strode across the beach toward the water's edge. Ridiculous to be impressed and yet...

"Take your shoes off," he said, and she shifted in his arms to do just that. Once she had them in her hands, he set her down, and Angela gasped at the feel of the cold, wet sand grabbing at her bare feet.

"Cold, huh?"

"Yeah," she said, and shrugged deeper into the folds of his sweatshirt. "But," she added, turning her face toward the incoming tide, "it's nice, too." It had been too long since she'd come here, she thought.

The full moon hung in a black sky, surrounded by the glitter of the stars. A wide, silvery path of moonlight stretched across the surface of the dark water and looked as though it led to the horizon and beyond—straight to Heaven. Here, in this spot, the rest of the world seemed very far away. It was as if she and Dan were alone on the edge of the universe. Even the lights and muted sounds from the pier couldn't disturb the intimate setting. "I love this place," she mused aloud. "I'd almost forgotten how much."

"Beautiful," he said softly, his voice just barely rising above the rush of the water as it slid across the sand, retaking the shoreline.

She inhaled deeply. "Yes, it is."

"I wasn't talking about the ocean."

That breath caught in her throat when Angela shot him a quick glance. His gaze was locked on her, and she knew that the whole time she'd been studying the beauty of nature, he'd been studying her. And though that should have worried her, a curl of pleasure unwound in the pit of her stomach, and a flash of heat swarmed up inside her to fight off the chill.

"Dan…"

"You're beautiful," he said, and lifted one hand out to smooth back a strand of her hair. His fingertips traced lightly across her cheek, and Angela closed her eyes in response. "Would you rather I didn't say it?"

"No, I—" She didn't know what she wanted. That was the problem. All she'd wanted from him was one night. One night to forget about her everyday life, her everyday world. But it was turning out to be something more, and she wasn't at all sure how to feel about that. Frustrated with her own indecision, she turned back to look at the ocean as she said, "I don't know."

He came up behind her and laid his hands on her

shoulders. She felt the hard, solid strength of his body aligned with hers, and Angela knew that nothing about this time with Dan would be simple.

"I don't want another husband," she blurted out, and winced when she heard the words aloud.

His hands tightened briefly on her shoulders before he said, "And I'm not applying for the job."

"I know that," she said, and if she'd been wearing her shoes, she would have kicked herself. Kicking herself barefoot wouldn't be worth the effort. "I just thought you should know how I feel. I'm not looking for a boyfriend..."

"I'm no boy," he reminded her.

No one knew that better than she did, she thought, still staring out at the ocean as if looking for someone to help her dig her way out of the hole she seemed to have fallen into. But there was no help to be found. "This is coming out all weird, but what I wanted you to know is that I'm not interested in a relationship."

"Fine," he said, and wrapped both arms around her, resting his chin on top of her head as they stared out at the moonlit water. "Now I know."

"Yeah." That was a good thing, right?

"You should know something, too."

"Okay." She braced herself for whatever was coming.

"I want to make love with you again. Now."

If she hadn't been leaning against him, she probably would have fallen over. Swallowing hard, she fought to speak past the roaring pulse of desire that threatened to choke her.

"Dan, I told you I didn't want a relationship—"

"Yeah? So?"

"So," she said, and lifted both hands to his arms. She felt the corded muscles bunched there and almost sighed. But she had to say this. "I'm not the kind of woman who takes lovers, either."

He chuckled, and she stiffened slightly as his breath ruffled her hair.

"What's so funny?"

"This whole conversation," he said, and turned her around in his grasp, waiting until she looked up into his eyes before he continued. "You *did* take a lover. Me. Last night."

Boy had she ever. Her body still tingled at the thought of his hands and tongue on her flesh. "I know but that was a one-time thing, and well…"

He shook his head and took her face between his palms. "It wasn't a one-time thing, Angel. It might not be forever, but it's sure as hell more than one night."

"I don't know what you want from me," she said, relishing the feel of his hands on her face, the soft stroke of his thumbs across her cheekbones.

"I don't want anything *from* you, Angel. I just want *you*."

The power of those words rocketed around inside her, and she wondered just how long it had been since she'd heard anything like them. Her own husband hadn't really wanted her. She'd been more of a convenience. Someone to cook and clean and take out his frustrations on by verbally abusing her.

But he hadn't *wanted* her. Not the way this man did. Not the way *she* wanted now. Those eyes of his, she thought, trembling inside. Oh, she was headed for trouble. No doubt by tomorrow morning she would be wishing she'd turned on her heel and run for safety. But tonight she didn't want to run from him. She wanted to run *to* him.

And then he kissed her, pulling her close, tilting her head and brushing his mouth across hers. Ripples of expectation spread and expanded within her. Gently, at first, his lips teased and taunted her, but within seconds the kiss deepened, strengthened. Angela dropped her shoes to the sand, wrapped her arms around his neck and went up on her toes to meet him.

Her blood singing, her heartbeat thundering in her ears, she parted her lips for the sweet invasion of his tongue, and when he'd entered her warmth, she sighed into his mouth, giving him her breath as well as her desire.

He held her tightly, firmly, his arms wrapped around her like twin bands of iron. Her breasts flattened against his chest, and her nipples ached with the want she knew he could ease.

A cold splash of water raced across the sand and splashed at her ankles and calves, and she gasped at the smack of yet another powerful sensation. Dan broke the kiss, smiled at her and asked, ''Your place? Before the tide comes in completely and washes us off the beach?''

Her lips still tingling from his kiss, her breath still laboring in and out of her lungs, Angela turned her brain off and let her emotions take control. Regrets could come later, she thought as she nodded and whispered, ''Let's go.''

He grabbed up her shoes, swung her up into his arms again and practically raced for the stairs. Angela's laughter floated in their wake and dissolved in the chill ocean air.

A bright, warm slash of sunlight lay across her eyes, prodding her into wakefulness when she would much rather have stayed asleep. She stretched, slowly, languidly, feeling the achy fatigue in every one of her muscles and smiling to herself at the memory of how she'd earned those aches.

She'd had no idea that sex could be...*fun.* Tense, passionate, sure. But fun? Images of the night before danced across her mind—the laughter, the tickling, the spontaneous wrestling match she'd almost won. She would be willing to bet neither of them had gotten more than an hour's sleep all night.

Wow.

Still smiling, she turned her head on the pillow, opened her eyes and looked at the man sleeping beside her. Even in rest, he looked...formidable, and so damn good. Stretching out one hand, she ran her fingertips gently along his cheek and was almost startled when his eyes flashed open.

"Good morning," he murmured, and the rumble of his voice rolled along her spine.

"Good morning," she said, amazed to feel the flicker of desire quickening inside her again. Good heavens, she thought, one weekend of passion and she'd created a monster! Angela Santini Jackson, The Lust Queen. How embarrassing was that?

He lifted one hand to stroke the length of her arm and she wanted nothing more than to move into his caress. But, fighting those instincts, Angela took a deep breath and rolled away to the edge of the bed. Her one night of passion had already become two. If she wasn't careful here, it could very possibly stretch into two nights and a day. Oh, my. If her sisters could see her now, they'd never believe it.

She glanced at the bedside clock, and when the actual time registered, she gasped. "Nine-thirty!" Leaping up off the bed, she raced naked across the room toward a tall, mahogany chest of drawers. Throwing him a quick look, she ordered, "You have to get up. Get dressed."

Dan rose up on one elbow, rubbed one hand across his face and asked, "What's the hurry?"

"Hurry?" A snort of choked laughter shot from her throat as she snatched up a pair of panties and slipped them on. Wrestling with a lacy bra next, she talked while she dressed. "Oh, it's only that Jeremy will be home any minute, expecting his traditional before-the-big-game breakfast."

"Oh," Dan said, nodding, and sat up, swinging his legs off the bed. "Do I have time for a shower?"

A shower? She glanced at the clock again and groaned. "With luck you might have time to get dressed!" Bending over, she grabbed his jeans from where he'd tossed them onto the floor the night before and threw them at him. "Hurry up. I don't want my son to see us...well, to wonder—" She broke off, slapped one hand to her forehead and muttered, "Oh, God, I'm so stupid. I'm a terrible person. A rotten mother, I should be shot...."

"Yeah," Dan said already pulling his clothes on. "You're right up there with the worst society has to offer all right."

She shot him a glare.

"Kidding," he said, holding up both hands.

"No time for jokes," she snapped, grabbing a bright-yellow T-shirt at random from a drawer.

"I get the picture," Dan said, and was dressed so quickly he finished before she did.

Slipping into a pair of loafers, Angela snatched her hairbrush off the top of her dresser and yanked it through her tangled hair. She didn't even wince at the pain, figuring she deserved it. "How did you do that?" she muttered. "Is it a Marine thing? Dressed and ready to move at a moment's notice?"

"Came in pretty handy today," he reminded her.

"True, true," she said, and dashed into the bathroom.

"How about I go down and make some coffee?" he called out.

She stuck her head through the doorway, shook her head and tried to say, despite the mouthful of toothbrush and toothpaste, "No. Jush go…"

"What?"

He was grinning at her! Clearly, he was enjoying her panic way too much.

"Go," she tried again, waving one hand at the bedroom door for emphasis. "I cah you ater."

Dan laughed at the frustration sparkling in her narrowed eyes. "I think the translation of that is that you'll call me later."

She nodded, gagged and dodged back into the bathroom to spit. "Yes," she said distinctly a moment later. "Now go away. Hurry!"

All right, he told himself. He'd go. He wouldn't embarrass her in front of her son. But he'd be back. Damned if he wouldn't—despite his better instincts warning him to stay clear of her. Despite the fact that neither of them wanted anything more permanent than a night's worth of magic.

He'd be back because he wasn't ready to say goodbye to Angela. Not yet.

And that one little fact scared the living hell out of him. But not enough to make him keep his distance, which was such a rare event, he hardly knew what to make of it himself.

He'd just closed the front door behind him when a car pulled into the driveway and an eight-year-old bundle of energy jumped out. Waving goodbye to his friend, Jeremy raced toward the front porch and skidded to a halt when he spotted Dan.

"Hey," the boy said, pointing at him. "I know you. You're my uncle Nick's friend."

"That's right," Dan said, smiling at the kid.

Jeremy's head tilted to one side as he stared at him. "What're you doing here?"

"Well..." Think fast, Mahoney.

The front door opened, and Angela stepped out, a grin of welcome on her face. But that grin shook a bit when she caught sight of Dan.

"Hi, Mom," her son said, taking the steps up to the porch. "Nick's friend is here. He was just about to knock on the door when I got here. Funny, huh?"

"Yeah," Angela said. "Quite a coincidence." She licked her lips and held out one hand toward Dan as if they were strangers. "Dan, isn't it?"

"That's right," he said, willing to play the game. He shook her hand and at the same time managed to stroke her palm with the tip of his index finger.

She jolted as if hit with a bolt of lightning and yanked her hand free of his grasp.

"What's he doin' here?" Jeremy asked, shrugging out of his backpack and tossing his dark-brown hair out of his eyes.

"Well…" Angela said slowly, obviously searching for a reason—any reason to explain Dan's presence.

"Actually," Dan spoke up quickly as an idea came to him. "At the wedding your mom was telling me all about what a great ballplayer you are, and I'm a big baseball fan, so I thought—"

Jeremy took a step toward him and gave him a wide, missing-one-front-tooth smile. "Y'mean you wanta go to my game?"

Dan lifted his gaze from Jeremy's excited features to Angela, standing just behind her son. Mutely, she shook her head and mouthed the word *no*.

She was right, of course. Neither of them needed the complication of dragging her son into the middle of whatever was happening between them. It would be best for all concerned if he just left as he'd planned to do before getting caught at the door. And he had every intention of doing just what she wanted.

Until he looked back down into Jeremy's eyes. Then he just couldn't do it. He remembered too well being the only kid on his baseball team without a parent in the stands. His father had been gone and his mother hadn't considered a Little League game worth her time.

Sure, Angela would be there for her son. But if

it made the kid feel better to know that there was someone else out there rooting for him, then that's what Dan had to do. Not just for Jeremy's sake but for his, too. For the memories of being a fatherless kid watching other boys his age laughing and talking with their dads.

Maybe it was a stupid thing to do. Okay, it *was* a stupid thing to do. He knew that. Just as he knew that he was going to do it, anyway.

"I sure do," he said, and from the corner of his eye, saw Angela's shoulders slump in defeat.

Her son, on the other hand, shouted, "Cool!"

Dan smiled and shrugged at the woman shooting daggers at him with her eyes.

"Jeremy," she said, laying one hand on his shoulder, "why don't you go in and get your uniform on before breakfast."

"Okay," the kid said, then shot another look at Dan.

"Mom always makes a Home Run breakfast for me before my games. Are you hungry?"

The boy took Dan's hand, dragging him through the door into the house. Looking back over his shoulder at the woman still standing on the porch, Dan let his gaze slide across her body head to toe before saying, "Kid, I'm starved."

Seven

Angela took another handful of popcorn and slid a covert look at the man beside her. Darned if he didn't look comfortable and right at home.

With his long legs stretched out on the bleacher seats in front of him, he leaned back, bracing his elbows on the seat behind him while he followed the action on the baseball diamond.

At first, she'd been angry that he'd somehow managed to wangle an invitation to join Jeremy and her for the day. She'd been sure he was simply using her son to get to her. But he hadn't made a pass at her all morning. Well, except for the heated looks she'd caught in his eyes a few times. And she figured she could hardly blame him for her over-the-top reaction to him.

He'd been a perfect gentleman toward her, while at the same time listening to everything Jeremy had to say, offering advice and in general, being...*nice*. It was awfully hard to stay mad at a man who was so kind to her son. And Jeremy was lapping it up like a rain-starved flower in a summer shower. It broke her heart to watch him, so eager for a man's attention.

But still. This couldn't work. Wouldn't work. She had to let him know in no uncertain terms that whatever they'd shared this weekend was officially at an end.

It wasn't safe—or fair to Dan—to let this go on. She wasn't interested in having a man in her life. She had Jeremy and that was enough. The two of them made a terrific team, and that's just how she wanted it to stay. Her sisters were both married now, thoughtfully providing Jeremy with the male role models he would be needing so desperately in the coming years. Her son would be happy, and as far as her love life went...well, she'd been celibate before, she could do it again.

Although, she thought, frowning slightly, she hadn't really minded the celibacy because she'd never really enjoyed sex. Until now. Now, thanks to this wild, wonderful weekend, she had a whole new appreciation for sex. And living without it might not be as easy as it had been before.

The last out of the inning was made, and the cheers from the parents who were sprinkled throughout the bleachers shattered her train of thought. Which was really just as well, she told herself. No point in getting depressed over something she couldn't change.

Jeremy's team ran in from the field to the dugout to get ready for their turn at bat. Dan sat up and applauded along with the rest of the appreciative crowd dotting the small, elementary-school diamond.

A soft wind blew in from the ocean, white clouds swirled across the morning sky, and the shouts of children filled the air. It was just the kind of day Angela usually enjoyed. Usually, she thought with another sidelong look at the man beside her.

"Hey, Mom!"

Forcing her thoughts aside for the moment, she followed the sound of that small voice and grinned at her son as he stared at her through the chain-link fence. "Hi, sweetie!" she called, and could have bitten her tongue off when she saw him wince in embarrassment.

"I'm up second," the boy said, and pushed the brim of his too-big batting helmet farther back on his forehead.

"That's great, Jer," she said, giving him a thumbs-up. "I'll be watching."

"Hey, Jeremy," Dan sat up and called out to the boy.

"Yeah?"

"You might want to try choking up on the bat a little."

Angela looked at him, but he wasn't paying any attention to her at all. Focused on the boy watching him, Dan went on.

"You know, scoot your hands farther up on the bat. It'll shorten your swing. Make it more powerful."

Jeremy frowned and shifted his small hands. "Like this you mean?"

Dan laughed. "Almost...here, let me show you." He pushed himself up, walked down the bleachers and around to the dugout entrance.

Angela watched them, man and boy and realized that, but for the once or twice her sister Marie's husband, Davis, had attended a game, this was the first time Jeremy had had a man around to show him the mysterious baseball secrets that were passed down from generation to generation. Keeping her gaze fixed on them, she watched Dan stand behind Jeremy, adjusting his stance, the position of his hands, the tilt of his head. And her son, the same little boy who argued any time his mother offered advice, was soaking it all in like a sponge.

Despite how nice it was of Dan to help her son out like this, it worried her that Jeremy seemed to be bonding with Dan so quickly. It couldn't be good for him, because Dan wouldn't be staying.

A twist of something sharp and painful settled around her heart, and not for the first time she wished that Jeremy had had the kind of father he'd deserved. But even before Bill died, he'd made it clear he wasn't interested in being involved with his son. Bill had never wanted kids and resented his son's existence. And even at five years old, Jeremy had been completely aware of his father's feelings. Hard not to be, when his every overture had been rebuffed.

She felt the telltale sting of tears welling in her eyes and hurriedly blinked them back. That time was over. For both her and Jeremy. They'd survived. They'd moved on. They were *happy,* damn it.

Now, watching Dan, a strong, confident man who'd been raised by a single mother, Angela was reassured that her son, too, could grow up fine without a father in his life.

A moment later Dan gave Jeremy's helmet a light tap, said something that made the boy laugh, then headed back to the bleachers. Once he was seated alongside her again, he said, "He really is a great kid, Angel."

"I know," she said, and heard the slight quaver in her voice.

So, apparently, had he. Swiveling his head to look at her, he asked, "Something wrong?"

"No," she started, then corrected herself and said what she'd been thinking, "I just don't think it's a good idea for you to get so friendly with Jeremy."

One dark eyebrow lifted. "Why not?"

Great. She'd offended him. Well, she would offend the Pope himself if she had to, to protect her son. "Because I don't want him to think you're always going to be around. I don't want him getting the idea that you and I are—"

"Are what?" he asked, his voice tight with a sudden flash of anger. "Friends?"

She laughed shortly, then gave a quick look around to make sure no one was close enough to listen in on the conversation. "Is that what we are? *Friends?*"

He sighed, and she watched the tension drain from him. She wasn't used to that. Whenever Bill was angry, he'd stayed that way for hours. He'd made the entire household miserable with his tantrums and had never been in a hurry to let go of his foul mood.

It seemed that here, too, Dan was different.

He reached for her hand, gave it a quick squeeze, then released her again. "Maybe we're a bit more than friends," he admitted quietly. "But we're certainly not less than that, are we?"

Images raced through her mind. Memories of laughter, passion, pleasure all came together to settle over her like a warm blanket. She'd known this man less than a week, and yet she somehow felt closer to him than she had to the man she'd married.

No, she didn't want a relationship. But was a

friendship such a bad thing? Would it be so dangerous to allow herself to have a friend who not only seemed to care for her, but was kind to her son? Jeremy, she thought, with a glance in his direction, was a child so hungry for the simple things shared between a father and a son. As she watched, the boy practiced his new stance and took a couple of swings with the bat, obviously pleased with himself.

"No," she said, more to herself than to Dan, "we're not less than friends."

His green eyes warmed, and he gave her a crooked half smile that was potent enough to curl her toes. She'd never had a friend who could do that to her before, so she knew they weren't simply friends.

What they were exactly, she wasn't sure. But now wasn't the time to think about it, she told herself firmly, dragging her gaze from Dan's. Now it was time to cheer for her son.

Jeremy strode to the plate, his bat balanced on his small shoulders, his helmet continually drooping down over his eyes. His little legs nearly swam in the uniform pants, and his tiny chin was tilted at a determined angle. Her son, she thought, feeling a rush of pure pride course through her. No matter how bad her marriage to Bill had been. No matter how unhappy they'd made each other, she would always be grateful to him for this perfect little boy.

He walked up to home plate, planted his small

feet in the batter's box and got ready. And just like every other time Jeremy took his turn at bat, she folded her hands together in her lap and said a quiet prayer. *Please, Lord, don't let him strike out. Just let him hit the ball. Just this once. Please?*

"Swing level, Jeremy," Dan called out from beside her and, chuckling, reached across to hold her still-clasped hands.

"You can do it, honey," Angela's voice lifted above the other shouts.

Jeremy swung.

And missed.

She groaned and squeezed Dan's hand tightly.

"It's okay, pal," he yelled. "You'll get the next one."

The boy nodded grimly, planted his feet more firmly in the dirt and waited for the pitch.

"Oh, I can't take this," she muttered thickly. It was horrible. All of this pressure on a little boy? It wasn't fair.

"You gonna close your eyes?" Dan asked.

"I want to," she admitted, and jerked with the slap of the ball into the catcher's mitt as Jeremy took another strike.

"Oh, man…" she muttered, already thinking about how disappointed Jeremy would be later.

Dan laughed gently. "You've got to relax, Mom."

"Easy for you to say."

"He can do it," Dan told her firmly.

"I know that, and you know that," she said softly, her gaze focused on her son and his challenge, "but does *he* know that?"

The pitcher wound up, reared back and let the ball fly. Angela's gaze followed it in. Jeremy swung the bat back then brought it forward in a hard, level motion. A *crack* of sound exploded as the ball smashed against the bat and sailed toward left field.

"Whooo-hooo!" Angela yelled, jumping up and down on the bleachers, shaking Dan's hands and watching her son as he tore off running down the first-base line. He rounded first and raced off toward second, all the while the left fielder chased that ball, finally taking off his mitt and throwing it at it. Jeremy made it to second standing up, and once he was safe on base, Angela turned around and leaped on Dan.

Arms wrapped firmly around his neck, she hugged him hard, then pulled her head back and grinned up into his smiling eyes. "He did it! He actually did it!"

"You're damn right he did," Dan said, and lifted one hand in a triumphant salute to the little soldier out on the playing field.

Still held in his embrace, Angela looked up at him and said simply, "Thank you."

"Always glad to help my friends," he said.

She nodded slowly, never taking her eyes from his. "Friends," she repeated, and wondered how many friendships had started in a bed.

* * *

The pizza place was packed to the rafters with Little Leaguers.

Dan took a bite of possibly the worst pepperoni pizza he'd ever had in his life and let his gaze drift across the crowded room. The noise level was worse than combat, what with the high-pitched shrieks and gales of laughter—not to mention the irritating background music that accompanied the singing chipmunks in a rock video blasting from a ten-foot screen in one corner. Bells and whistles erupted at regular intervals from the row of arcade games along the walls. And somewhere in the place a trio of waiters were singing "Happy Birthday" in loud, off-key voices.

It was enough to drive anyone but the most doting parent right over the edge. And Dan hadn't had so much fun since he was a Drill Instructor.

At the table opposite him, Jeremy's team sat victorious, chowing down bad pizza and burned fried chicken and slurping at sodas poured by their proud, smiling moms. They were filthy, tired and filled with enough energy to make a Navy SEAL team look like slackers.

It made Dan tired just watching them. His gaze shifted to Jeremy just in time to watch him get another congratulatory slap on the back. The kid had gotten three solid base hits during the game, and he was practically glowing with pride.

"Terrible, isn't it?" Angela shouted as she

stepped over the bench seat and sat down beside him.

"What?" he called back.

"The pizza," she said loudly. "It's the worst."

"Hideous," he agreed, and dropped his slice back onto his plate. Pushing that plate aside, he leaned one elbow on the table and half turned to face her. "So why are we here?"

She laughed, and something inside Dan twisted into a strangling knot. Damn, she was beautiful. From her wind-tousled dark hair to the fathomless depths of her brown eyes.

"Tradition," she told him. "Bad pizza or not, this is the place to go after a game."

Well nobody understood tradition better than a Marine. Nodding toward the other table, he said, "Jeremy sure looks like he's enjoying himself."

"Are you kidding?" she asked, laying one hand on his arm. "He's in seventh heaven!" Then giving him a light pat, she added, "Thanks to you."

"Me?" he asked, glancing down at her hand on his arm.

"You showed him how to hit." Leaning in close, she kissed his cheek, then sat back. "Thank you."

His skin actually seemed to be sizzling. One little kiss shouldn't be affecting him like this. But it was more than the kiss and he knew it. Damn, this woman had something no one else he'd ever known possessed. But he didn't want her gratitude. He wanted...hell. He wasn't sure exactly what it was he wanted.

Which made for a potentially cranky Marine.

"No big deal," he said, trying to brush her thanks aside.

"It was to him," Angela said. "And to me."

Okay, now he was uncomfortable.

"Hey!" Jeremy had somehow slipped up on them and was now tugging at the sleeve of Dan's T-shirt.

Reprieve, he thought, and almost grimaced at the cowardly thought.

"Hey, yourself," Dan said, then had to laugh at the kid's dirty face and eager expression.

"You want to play a game?" he asked, grinning and showing off that gap left by a missing tooth.

"Jeremy," Angela spoke up, still yelling to be heard, "why don't you play with your friends."

Her son shot her a look that clearly said, *This is guy business,* before turning back to Dan. "You like bowling? You know the kind where you roll the little ball up into the rings for points?"

"Don't think I ever played it," Dan said, giving Angela a smile.

"No way!" The boy was appalled. "It's really cool and you can win lots of great stuff. Come on, I can show you."

"You don't have to," Angela said apologetically as he stood up.

"I know," Dan told her. "I want to." And as he

followed the kid through the maze of short people in baseball uniforms, he realized that was nothing less than the truth.

Who would have guessed that Dan No-Strings-Attached-Mahoney would actually be having a good time in a kiddie arcade?

He threw a quick look over his shoulder at Angela, and when their gazes locked, he knew without a word passing between them that there would be other, more adult, games played later that night.

Eight

But there were no more games later.

Dan stood at the bottom of the porch steps, watching the screen door slam behind Jeremy as the boy raced inside, his shouted, "'Bye!" still echoing in the afternoon air.

Turning to the woman standing beside him, Dan reached out and brushed her hair back from her face. She shivered, ducked her head, then lifted it again to meet his gaze with hers.

"Thanks for coming today," she said softly. "Jeremy really enjoyed it."

"So did I," he said, just as quietly.

"Yeah, me, too."

A few silent minutes passed between them, with

the only sound that of a lawn mower purring in the distance.

He looked into her eyes and tried to think of something to say. Some way to explain the strangeness of what he was feeling. Thinking. But he came up empty, and it was just as well, because she started speaking a moment later.

"Look, Dan," Angela said, casting one quick look at the front door to make sure her son wasn't overhearing her, "this weekend was really…" Her voice trailed off as she searched for the right word and couldn't find it.

"Yeah," he said, "it was."

Nodding, she inhaled sharply, shoved her hands into her jeans pockets and continued. "But I don't want you to think that I expect—or want—anything more. I mean—" She stopped and shook her head. "I don't know what I mean."

"I know the feeling," he muttered, and didn't know if it made him feel better or worse, knowing that Angela was just as confused as he was.

"I'm not used to this, you know," she said abruptly.

"This?"

"Casual…*flings,*" she said, frowning at the word. "Look, you're a nice guy, and I had an incredible time with you, but—"

"But what?" he asked, his voice sounding tight even to him. Okay, the day kept getting weirder. He'd awakened in bed beside a beautiful woman he'd made love to all night. Then he'd spent most of the day surrounded by munchkins and talking chipmunks. He'd eaten bad pizza, lost at skeet bowling and now was about to be dumped.

Damn it.

"I'm a *mom,*" she told him, yanking her hands free and throwing them wide for emphasis. "I just can't do the casual thing."

"Didn't stop you yesterday," he reminded her. "Or this morning."

A flush of heat swept up into her cheeks, making her eyes seem darker, deeper. And Dan had to admit the blush endeared her to him. He would have bet cold, hard cash there wasn't a woman alive in today's modern world who could still blush.

"I know," she said, and folded her arms around her middle. "But that was different."

"How?"

"It was an aberration," she said softly. "One weekend out of my life."

"It doesn't have to be just the one weekend," he said, and could hardly believe his own ears. Was this really *him* talking? Hell, ordinarily he'd be heading for the hills by now. Ordinarily he never would have spent the whole night beside her, holding her, watching her sleep. He had cheated himself of that closeness in order to keep from caring. But this time, with this woman, he hadn't been able to help himself.

"Yes it does," she said quietly, her gaze delving deeply into his.

Something twisted around his heart and squeezed. Dan reached out to cup her cheek, and briefly she turned her face into his palm. Then she stepped back and away from him, shaking her head.

"I'm sorry, Dan. This is just how it has to be."

"Angela—"

"Goodbye," she said, and before he could speak again, she turned, ran up the steps and into the house. Then she closed and locked the door, shutting him out.

Alone on the walkway, Dan stared at the house for a long minute, then turned toward his car. Frowning thoughtfully to himself, he wondered why he wasn't celebrating his neat escape from a too-tender trap.

It had been a fun weekend—okay, better than fun—fantasy time. But now the real world had swung back into place and it was time for her to forget about her walk on the wild side.

A curl of something warm and delicious unwound inside her, and Angela squirmed uncomfortably in the driver's seat. Easier said than done, she thought, and instantly Dan Mahoney's face popped into her mind.

Those green eyes of his. That smile. Those hands.

The warmth increased until she was forced to roll

down the window and stick her head out, hoping the morning breeze off the nearby ocean would be cold enough to cool her blood. But to do that she would need an ice storm, and judging by the blue sky overhead, there wasn't one headed her way.

"Oh, man…"

She shoved one hand through her hair and stared at the house as she waited for her perpetually late son to come and join her for the ride to school. Monday morning. Classes to teach, work to get accomplished, son to raise. All of the everyday, ordinary parts of her life. So why did it all feel so different today? Why did *she* feel so different?

Sex?

Could a couple of evenings of amazing sex really have such an effect on a person? Well, obviously yes. But even she didn't entirely believe that. It hadn't been just sex. It had been more. So much more it had scared her.

There was a connection between Dan Mahoney and her that she not only didn't want, but intended to ignore completely. Why was nothing simple for her? Other women were able to briefly find a little adult, mutually satisfying pleasure without worrying about guilt or responsibilities. Why couldn't she?

"Oh, stop it," she muttered, glancing into her rearview mirror. Frowning at herself, she went on in a stern lecture to the woman in the glass. "You're making too much out of this, y'know. It's not like Dan went down on one knee and professed his undying love, for Pete's sake.'' She nodded and, since she was being so convincing, went on. ''You both had a good time and now it's over. So stop thinking about him already!''

The passenger door opened and Jeremy asked, ''Who you talkin' to, Mom?''

She jumped, startled, and shot her bouncing baby boy a look. ''No one,'' she said, then as he slid onto his seat, asked, ''did you lock the front door?''

''Oops!'' He threw her a sheepish grin that looked so much like his father's, Angela drew in a sharp breath. ''I'll be right back,'' he said, and raced toward the house again.

Strange, the warmth that had crept inside her at thoughts of Dan was gone now. And all it had taken was that brief reminder of her late husband. Watching Jeremy run up the porch steps, Angela remembered how it had been with Bill in the beginning.

He'd been her first...her only...lover—until this past weekend—and when he'd touched her, she'd felt all the magic, all the promise of new love. It was a dim memory now, but if she tried hard enough, Angela could remember the anxious fumbling in the dark, the quickened breathing, the heart-stopping fear mingled with excitement and risk.

Yes, it had been good with Bill those first few times, because she'd loved him. Because she wasn't old enough or experienced enough to know that he was a selfish lover because he was a selfish man. And then she'd become pregnant with Jeremy and almost before the pregnancy test results were dry, she'd found herself hurriedly married to a man who had never stopped resenting her for "ruining his life."

So much for magic.

The front door slammed, shattering her images of the past. As she watched Jeremy run toward her, his gap-toothed grin firmly in place, Angela told herself that the only reason she'd found so much joy and pleasure with Dan was because it was new. Because it had been so long since she'd felt anything.

And she wouldn't risk making another mistake in the Love Game. Not when this time she wouldn't be the only one to pay the price. Jeremy slid into his seat, slammed the car door and buckled his seat belt. She reached out to smooth his hair down and made a silent promise that she would *never* do anything that might wipe that smile away. She would keep him safe and happy even if it meant she lived the rest of her life alone.

"Okay, relax," Angela said hours later as Jeremy practically vibrated in his seat.

"I'm almost late," her son accused, shooting her a look that clearly read, *Hurry up, Mom.*

She waited for oncoming traffic to pass before making a left turn into the Bayside Park parking lot. She'd had a long day, dealing with third-graders who simply weren't interested in multiplication tables or history for that matter. And all she wanted now was a little peace and quiet.

Sighing, she pointed out, "You do realize that *almost late* actually means *on time?*"

"Mo-om," her pride and joy groaned.

How did children manage to draw out a one-syllable word until it sounded as long as supercalifragilisticexpialidocious?

Still sighing, she pulled into one of the diagonal slots, threw the gearshift into Park and turned off the engine. Jeremy already had his door open and one foot out when she stopped him.

"No kiss?" she asked, feigning a deep, personal injury.

"The guys are over there," he muttered with a shake of his head.

"Forgive me," she said, properly chastised. Honestly, it was hard to keep up with him anymore. One minute he was her little boy and the next, he was too cool for words.

"Later, okay?"

She grinned at him. "Later for sure."

"Okay." He hopped out of the car, then looked back in at her. "Are you gonna watch practice?"

"Do you want me to?" she asked.

"I guess it'd be all right," he allowed. "Some of the other guys' moms come to watch."

"Well, good, then I will, too," she assured him.

Actually, she'd already been planning on staying for his baseball practice. She had a stack of papers to grade and besides, she really didn't want to go back home to sit in the house all alone and brood. Because she definitely *would* brood. Thoughts of Dan Mahoney had plagued her all day. Not even one of her students throwing up during English class had been enough to distract her.

She'd done the right thing by ending what was between them before it could get started. But that didn't mean she had to be happy about it. Or that she wouldn't think about him from time to time, to time to time…oh, for heaven's sake.

"Hey," Jeremy crowed, and Angela looked up to see what had her son sounding as though he'd just found a ten-dollar bill.

She followed his gaze to the practice field where twelve boys and girls were gathered around their coaches.

Coaches?

Since when had Jeremy's team had more than one official coach? No one had been willing to volunteer the time to help Joe Cassaccio run the team. So who else was out there now? A thread of suspicion slipped through her as, frowning to herself, Angela squinted at the men talking to the kids.

There was Joe, a tall, muscle-bound man with kind eyes and a warm heart, and beside him— A sinking sensation started in the pit of her stomach and wobbled right down to her knees. No way.

"He came," Jeremy said, disbelief coloring his voice. "He really came, just like he said he would."

Slowly she swiveled her head to look at her oh-so-innocent son. "What do you mean," she asked, "'just like he said'?"

Hopping from foot to foot in excitement, Jeremy was clearly torn between answering his mother and tearing out to the field to say hello to his new coach, Dan Mahoney.

"Yesterday at the pizza place I told him how Coach could really use some help and how nobody wanted the job and how I wouldn't mind at all if *he* wanted to do it, since he knew so much about hitting and all, and how he really helped me and how the other guys really liked him and—" He finally ran out of breath and paused for another. "But I didn't know if he'd really do it or not, but there he is!"

Yep, she thought, her gaze shifting back to the man whose body she'd spent two glorious days exploring, there he is.

"Isn't this *cool?*" Jeremy asked no one in particular just before slamming the car door and running across the field.

"Oh, yeah," she muttered to herself as she gathered up her things and stepped out of the car. "This is just the coolest."

Dan looked up as Jeremy ran toward them, and he smiled at the kid's obvious excitement. When the boy came to a skidding stop right beside him, Dan laid one hand on his shoulder and gave it a squeeze. The kid was practically vibrating.

And damned if it didn't feel good to know that he'd been able to do this for the boy. Okay, so he'd never actually planned on being a Little League coach. He knew baseball as well as the next guy. How hard could it be?

Then his gaze shifted toward the woman walking across the field, and he had the answer to his unspoken question. Even at a distance he could see anger pulsing out all around her. Well, he supposed he couldn't really blame her. But he hadn't agreed to be a coach just to see her. Sure it was a nice plus, but the real reason behind his decision was Jeremy.

The kid reminded him too much of himself at that age: only child of a single mother; no dad in the house or even in the picture. He remembered all too well how it felt to crave the company of men. To want to have one man to look up to. To model himself after.

Well, maybe he wasn't the best role model in the world, Dan thought, but he wasn't the worst, either.

The head coach spoke up suddenly, and Dan shifted his gaze to Joe.

"Well, kids, now that you've all met our new assistant coach," the man said, "why don't you go out and do some warming up before practice?"

The group of jeans-clad kids whooped and took off at a sprint, while Joe shouted after them, "Pitchers, I want you at the plate. We need to work on your windups." Then he looked at Dan and smiled. "Thanks again. I can really use the help."

"My pleasure," Dan told him, and surprisingly enough, meant it.

"See you out there."

Joe trotted off toward the pitchers, leaving Jeremy and Dan alone for a minute.

"I can't believe you really did it," the boy said.

Dan went down into a crouch so he could look the kid in the eye. "I said I would, didn't I?"

"Well, yeah, but—"

"I keep my promises, Jeremy," he said, reaching out to tap the brim of the boy's hat down over his eyes. "That's why I'm so careful about making them."

Clutching his baseball mitt, Jeremy pushed his hat back up and nodded. "I get it," he said.

"Good, now get on out there and warm up."

"Yes, sir!" He took off at a dead run to join his friends just as his mother came to a stop in front of Dan.

"What are you doing?" she asked shortly.

Slowly he stood up, tucking his hands into the back pockets of his jeans. His gaze drifted up and down her body before settling on her eyes. "I'm helping to coach a baseball team."

"I can see that."

"Then why'd you ask?" He smiled at her, but she didn't smile back. Ah, well.

"That's not what I meant and you know it."

"Angel…"

"Angela."

"Fine. Angela."

"Dan, why are you here?" she asked, keeping her voice low, despite the fact that no one was close enough to hear them. "We talked about this yesterday. I told you I couldn't—you know."

"This isn't about you, Angela," he said simply. "It's not about us."

"Then why?" she demanded, plucking her wind-blown hair out of her eyes and fixing her gaze on him.

Sighing, he turned and pointed toward the group of kids now running back and forth between first and second base. Jeremy was out in front and clearly determined to stay there. "Because of him," he said quietly.

"Jeremy?"

"That's right."

She clutched a stack of papers to her chest, shook her hair back out of her face and said, "You expect me to believe you would volunteer to help coach a baseball team because of a boy you hardly know?"

He rubbed the back of his neck and told himself to keep calm. Hell, he'd known she wouldn't be happy. He'd been expecting this. But still…why did she have to make it sound like he was some kind of liar?

"I don't *expect* you to believe anything, Angel," he said, using the nickname deliberately. "But whether you do or not, Jeremy's the reason I'm here."

She didn't look convinced. But there was more than anger in her eyes. There was suspicion and hurt. Maybe other men had tried to use her son to get to her, but he'd be damned if he'd be burned because of another man's actions.

Lowering his voice, he took her elbow and turned her away from the crowd of kids on the diamond. Then, looking directly into her eyes, he said, "I told you that I see a lot of myself in that kid of yours…."

"Yes, but—"

"No buts, Angel," he said tightly, "this has *nothing* to do with you. This is between me and Jeremy."

She stared into his eyes and seemed to be searching for assurances he couldn't give her. Finally, though, she said, "I wish I could believe that."

"Do or don't, Angel," he snapped, at last giving in to the anger simmering inside. "I can't help you with that. Right now I've got Little League practice."

Then he marched off as if he was on the parade

ground, and didn't look back. Didn't dare look back. Because one more glance into those wounded eyes of hers and he would end up making a damned fool of himself.

Nine

Angela sat on the bleachers, and though she tried to work through the stack of badly lettered spelling tests on her lap, her gaze kept shifting to the baseball diamond.

For two hours the coaches ran the kids' little legs off. There was practice at batting, fielding, sliding and catching. There was running and sprinting and thanks to Dan's Marine training, even some calisthenics. And the kids loved it.

Especially, she duly noted, her son.

Angela's gaze drifted toward the spot where Jeremy and Dan worked together to improve the boy's batting stance. The look on her son's face was priceless—and dismaying. He stared up at Dan as though he was a mixture of Babe Ruth, Santa Claus and God.

She sighed heavily and realized that no matter what else happened from here on out, there would be heartache waiting for her son at the end of it. But for now, she thought, watching Dan ruffle Jeremy's hair with one big hand, her little boy was in Heaven.

Dan looked up then, his gaze meeting hers, and for just an instant she felt a simmer of heat snake through her body and light a fire at her center. One look, she thought. One look from those eyes of his, and her body actually melted.

"Mom!"

She blinked and shook away thoughts that had no business at all invading her mind. Looking toward the sound of Jeremy's voice, she saw him, fingers clutching at the chain-link fence, face pressed against the metal until his skin looked as though it was checkered.

"What?" she asked with a laugh.

"Can Dan have dinner with us?" he asked, and before she could shout *No!*, he pulled out the big guns. *"Please?"*

She lifted her gaze to the man standing just behind the boy. Dan held both hands high and shook his head as if disclaiming any responsibility for this situation.

Like she believed that.

"Come on, Mom," Jeremy pleaded again. "He said he'd show me Pete Rose's batting stance."

Dan shrugged and gave her a half smile.

She sighed and dropped her gaze to Jeremy again. She was beaten and she knew it. She could no more look into those hopeful eyes and say no than she could sprout wings and fly around the infield.

"Pete Rose, huh?" she said in all seriousness. "Well, why didn't you say so? Of *course* Dan can come to dinner, then."

Jeremy naturally missed the sting of sarcasm in her words, but it was plain from Dan's expression that he hadn't. Good. Maybe he would decline and save them all a lot of grief.

She should have known better.

"A gracious invitation," he said with a smile that jump-started her heart, "I accept."

"All right!" Jeremy crowed, and took off toward the other players.

"Yippee," Angela muttered, but no one was listening.

And so it went. For the next week, every time she turned around, Dan was there. At practice, at the house, sitting at the kitchen table, laughing with her son, making himself such a part of the boy's life…and hers, she knew she had to do something fast—stop all of this before it went too far.

The problem was that she had a feeling it had

already gone too far. For her—as well as Jeremy. She'd caught herself looking for Dan at the baseball field. Listening for the sound of his voice. Cooking things she knew he'd like. Wishing they had just an hour alone to rekindle the amazing sensations they'd experienced together the week before.

Her body ached for his touch, and her dreams were filled with too-vivid images of him. Somehow her harmless idea of a one-night stand with a gloriously sexy man had developed into…what? Yet another problem. She wasn't sure what it was that lay between her and Dan Mahoney.

And with Mama still off on her cruise, she, Jeremy and Dan had settled into a comfortable little routine, which could only blow up in their faces as soon as it all ended. As she knew it would.

Soon enough, Mr. Love-'em-and-leave-'em would do just that.

Which was the main reason she'd decided to have a little chat with Dan tonight.

Jeremy had chattered all through dinner, for which Angela was eternally grateful. And after surviving the longest meal in the history of the world, she'd kept busy by taking twice as long as usual to clean the kitchen.

But when the room nearly glistened in the overhead lights, she realized she'd put the inevitable off as long as she possibly could. Tossing the dish towel onto the counter, she flipped off the light and walked into the living room.

The familiar room looked—even *felt*—different, she thought as she paused in the archway and leaned against the doorjamb. She was used to the cozy feel of the living room, with its overstuffed chairs and matching sofas, friendly clutter of magazines strewn across the coffee table and wide windows that looked out onto the front yard. But for the past week, it had seemed different because Dan was there. A man she'd slept with, made love with…and still wanted, heaven help her.

In the flickering light of the television set, Jeremy and Dan laughed together over a plate of cookies and hardly noticed when she walked in behind them. Her son, she thought, looked desperately happy to have the one-on-one attention of an obviously nice man. Had he really been so lonely for male company?

Well, if he was, she'd just have to see to it that Marie's and Gina's husbands spent more time with him. Because after the talk she planned to have with Dan tonight, it was a safe bet that he wouldn't be hanging around much longer.

"Bedtime," she said, and laid both hands on the back of the sofa, her fingers curling into the soft, worn fabric.

"Aw, Mom," Jeremy groaned, tearing his gaze from Dan's to look with pleading eyes up at his mother.

"Forget it," she said, shaking her head. "No reprieves tonight. You've got school in the morning and that means you need plenty of sleep tonight.''

''Man…''

''You heard your mom, recruit,'' Dan said with a smile. ''Move out.''

The boy snapped a clumsy salute and said, ''Aye-aye, First Sergeant.'' Then he hopped off the couch, came around the end and reached up to give his mother a kiss.

Angela kissed him and whispered, ''I'll be up to say good-night in a little while.''

It had been a long time since Jeremy had accepted bedtime without a battle. And it didn't do her the least bit of good to know that his willingness to comply this last week was due more to Dan's influence than hers.

Which only served to underline the importance of having a little ''chat'' with the man now watching her with a hungry light in his eyes. Her stomach skittered, and she pulled in a deep breath to try to ease the sudden tension stirring within her. It didn't work. She had a feeling nothing would. But that didn't change what had to be said.

He was becoming too much a part of their lives. Too entwined in the daily fabric of their routine. And she couldn't let that happen.

''Dinner was good,'' he said softly.

''Thanks,'' she whispered, tossing a quick look over her shoulder to make sure Jeremy had gone to his room.

"Why don't you come sit down for a minute?" Dan patted the sofa cushion beside him.

Curl up beside him on the couch, just the two of them, alone in the dim light? Oh, she wanted to. Desperately. For a week now, she'd settled for a touch on her hand, a kiss on her cheek. Always, always, he'd left right after Jeremy went to bed, as if unwilling to start something he couldn't finish with her son in the house.

And she'd been grateful. And tortured. If she joined him on that couch now, she just knew her self-control would melt away in the blink of an eye.

At the thought of his hands and mouth on her, she swallowed hard, shook her head and muttered thickly, "I don't think that's a good idea."

"I don't bite," he said with a smile as he pushed up from the couch and walked around it toward her.

"Not how I remember it," she whispered, and knew she'd said it loud enough to be overheard when she saw the quick smile lift one corner of his mouth.

"Well," he said quietly, "what's a bite or two between friends?"

A swarm of bees took off in her stomach. "Oh, my."

Looking up into his eyes, she fought down the sensation and ignored her own urge to lean into him. Casting another quick look at the hallway that led to Jeremy's room, she said, "Jeremy…"

"He's in his room," Dan said softly, and reached out to smooth his palm down the length of her arm.

She shivered and took a step back. "No," she said, as much to herself as to him. "No, I can't do this."

"We're not *doing* anything," he said, his voice a low rumble of sound in the shadowy room. "And I wouldn't try. Not with your son around."

That didn't change the fact that she *wanted* him to, Angela thought, steeling her spine and taking a firm grip on what was left of her willpower. "Dan, you have to go."

He took a breath then nodded. "All right."

"And you can't come back," she added.

He froze and looked at her. "Look, Angel," he said, "I know it's a little awkward, me spending so much time here and all—"

"That's not what I have a problem with," she said, and took a hasty step back, preferring to keep a safe distance between them.

He noticed and frowned slightly before folding his arms across his chest, planting his feet in a wide stance and tipping his head to one side to study her. "All right, then let's have it. What is the problem?"

"Where do I begin?" she whispered, more to herself than to him.

"How about at the beginning?"

The beginning. The wedding rehearsal when she'd first seen him. First hatched the ridiculous plan to seduce him, use him, then go back into her cloistered life. No, she wasn't going there.

Shoving both hands through her hair, she just managed to resist squeezing her skull between her palms. She let her hands drop to her sides, then shoved them into her jeans pockets. Stalling wouldn't help, she thought. She just had to say it, flat-out.

"You know what the problem is as well as I do."

"No, I don't think I do. Why don't you tell me?" he asked, and she noticed the tightness in his voice.

Well, fine. It'd be safer for both of them if anger took the place of lusty feelings.

"You coming here," she said, reminding herself again to keep her voice down. "Being Jeremy's coach, having dinner with us, creating these cozy little scenes—" Her voice broke off and she swallowed hard.

"Scenes?" he repeated, and she watched storm clouds flash across his eyes. "You think I set this up? Like some kind of play?"

"No," she said, disgusted with herself for not being able to make herself clear. So she wasn't very good at this whole confrontation thing. She hadn't had much practice. And it showed. This wasn't going at all well. And she had no one to blame but herself. No doubt she'd gone about it all wrong. After all, what had he really done that was so awful? Been kind to her son? Given her enough memories of passion to last her a lifetime?

Oh, yeah, she thought grimly. The rotten guy. Stand him up against a wall and shoot him.

Then he was talking again, and Angela had to force herself to pay attention.

"You're selling your kid short if you think I'm using him to get to you."

"I didn't say that," she countered. Hadn't really believed it, either, even when the thought had flashed briefly through her mind.

"You were thinking it."

"You read minds?" she snapped, ignoring the sharp teeth of guilt gnawing at her insides. "Must come in handy when you're out invading small countries."

Dan shoved one hand across the top of his head, whooshed out a breath and glared at the woman staring him down. Hardheaded female. She tilted her chin, narrowed her eyes, and Dan got set for what was coming.

Okay, maybe he couldn't blame her for being a little snippy. But damn it, he wouldn't be accused of using a child. You'd think over the past week or so she'd have gotten to know him a little better than that.

"I don't want Jeremy getting hurt."

Stung, he asked, "You really think I'd do anything to hurt that kid?"

She blinked at the harsh, abrupt tone. "No. Not deliberately, anyway."

"That's some consolation, I guess," he whispered, more to himself than to her. Then, staring directly into her eyes, he strove for his last bit of patience and said again, "I told you before, Angela, this isn't about you and me. It's about Jeremy."

"He's my son," she reminded him. "Anything that concerns Jeremy concerns me."

"I know that," he said, trying to control the rush of frustration still building inside. She was right, and no one knew that better than he. Hadn't he lived through the succession of men who'd come to see his mother? Hadn't he hated them all and resented her?

Hell, of course Angela worried about her son. That's one of the things he liked best about her. Scrubbing one hand across the back of his neck, he ducked his head, then looked up at her again. He was out of his depth, and he knew it. He hadn't meant for any of this to happen, damn it. He'd never counted on *caring* for her or Jeremy.

And now that he did, he wasn't entirely sure what to do about it.

So what was wrong with him, anyway?

For a solid week now he'd been rushing through his duties on base and then racing out to a Little League diamond. He'd found himself looking forward to small family dinners and a night of television. The guys he normally played poker with three times a week thought he'd died and even the Colonel had commented that Dan seemed distracted lately.

Distracted was a mild word for it.

Angela Santini Jackson should have been no more than a warm body on a cold night. He'd expected nothing more, and maybe that's why he'd been surprised to find so much. And why the thought of leaving cut him to the bone.

She stopped tapping her toe against the rug, and silence settled down hard. She took a long, deep breath and met his gaze squarely. "I know you probably mean well," she said.

"Gee," he countered with heartfelt sarcasm. "Thanks."

She ignored that. "I don't want what's between us to affect Jeremy."

"It doesn't have to."

"Doesn't it?" she demanded. "Hasn't it already? He's made you into his Little League coach for heaven's sake."

"That was my decision," he said. Granted, he'd made it on the spur of the moment, while looking into a small boy's wide, brown eyes and gap-toothed grin. But damned if he hadn't been having a good time at it.

"And Jeremy's enjoying it…*now*." She wrapped her arms around her middle and hung on. "But don't you see? I don't want him counting on you to be around. It's not right. Not fair to him."

She wanted him to leave. To fade away as though he'd never been there. And maybe that's what he should do. But it wasn't what he *would* do.

"I made a promise," he said flatly.

"I can explain to him—"

"What?" he cut her off, giving in to the snap and snarl of anger bubbling inside.

"Lower your voice," she said, throwing a look at the hallway behind her.

He did. "What can you explain, Angel? That a man he thought of as a friend didn't think enough of him to keep a promise?"

"He'll understand," she said, but didn't sound convinced.

"No, he won't," Dan told her, and took a step closer. She wanted to back up, he saw it in her eyes. But she didn't, and he gave her points for standing her ground. Just as he would stand his. "You know how I know that?" he asked, lowering his voice and bending his head down until they were nearly at the same level. "Because I used to *be* him. I was that kid. The kid with no dad. A kid with a handful of broken promises from men who passed through my mother's life."

Memories swirled up inside his mind, and he fought them down, but not before old stings and old fears came clear enough to shake him. How many times, he wondered, had he heard his mother say, *All men are bastards, son. You will be, too, one day. You can't help it. Sooner or later, you'll hurt the one you love.*

It was the main reason he'd steered clear of entanglements. Why he'd allowed himself no more connection than brief encounters with women as uninterested in tomorrow as he. He'd promised himself a long time ago to never be the man his father had been.

Yet now he stood in danger of being that man.

Taking her upper arms in a firm but gentle grip, he pulled her close, forcing her to look up at him. Staring down into those soft-brown eyes, he felt something inside him shift, tighten. "See, Angel," he said quietly, squeezing the words past the knot in his throat, "you try, but you don't know. You don't know what it's like to be waiting for someone who never shows up. You don't know what it's like to stop believing."

"Yes, I do," she said, laying her palms flat against his chest. "Jeremy's father never kept a promise in his life. Not to Jeremy. Not to me. So I know exactly how it feels to wait. To be forgotten."

"Then how can you expect me to do that to your son?"

She pushed away from him, took a step back and flung her hair out of her eyes with an angry toss of her head. "I don't want him hurt."

"Neither do I," Dan said, and meant it. He'd already come to care for the little guy. "And I won't be the one to hurt him by breaking a promise just to make you more comfortable."

"You don't get to decide this, Mr. Almighty-Marine…" Shaking her index finger at him, she said in an almost whisper, "When we first met, I told you I wasn't looking for a knight in shining armor. I don't need you to swoop in and lord it all over us.''

"Lady," he murmured, "you're unbelievable."

She folded her arms over her chest in a classically defensive posture.

"I'm no damn knight and I'm not lookin' to slay your dragons for you." He took a step closer and loomed over her, forcing her to tilt her head way back just to meet his gaze. "But I don't give my word lightly, Angel. And when I do, I keep it."

A long, tense moment of quiet passed before she pushed one hand through her hair and muttered, "This wasn't supposed to happen."

"What?"

"Us," she said, shooting him a look that plainly said she blamed him for this whole mess. "It was supposed to be one night."

"What do you mean?" he asked, pretty sure he wouldn't like the answer.

She shook her head. "Everyone told me you were a one-night-stand guy. I thought, I figured..."

He inhaled sharply as her words hit him like bullets. "You figured we'd have a good time and then I'd disappear."

"Well," she said, inhaling sharply, then blowing it out again, "yes."

"Sorry to disappoint you," he said, and felt an unexpected sharp slash of pain gouge at him. Why her words should hurt, he couldn't say. They were no more than the truth. For years that had been exactly who he was. And he supposed it was some sort of weird Karmic justice that the one time he was tempted to want more from a woman was the one time the woman wasn't interested.

Something cold and hard and heavy settled around his heart. And *that* feeling he was used to.

"I wasn't expecting this," she muttered furiously.

"Yeah," he said shortly. "Neither was I."

"Dan—"

"No, you're right," he said, interrupting whatever else she might have said. "This shouldn't have happened. I shouldn't have let it."

"There're two of us here, y'know," she reminded him.

He ignored that. This was his fault. He never should have stuck around. Never should have let himself care. He looked into her eyes again and knew that no matter how long he lived, he would always see those eyes and the shadows of what might have been. But reality was a hard fist in the gut, and he reacted to it. The only sure way to protect her from him was to walk away. Now, while the pain was still bearable.

"I do care for you," he said tightly. "And that's why I'm leaving."

"What?"

"It's better this way," he said, snatching up his jacket from the couch and shoving his arms into the sleeves. "My mother was right. Eventually I'll become the bastard I'm destined to be. I don't want to hurt you, but I probably would."

"What are you talking about?"

He gave her a brief smile and shook his head. "Doesn't matter. It's history. Like us." Then, walking to the door, he opened it, stepped out onto the porch and closed it quietly behind him.

He crossed the porch and went down the steps, walking into the bite of the cold night air. As he moved deeper into the darkness, he knew he was leaving behind the only *real* light he'd ever known.

Ten

Angela nearly snarled at the ringing phone. After a long, sleepless night, she wasn't in the best possible mood. She lifted her head off the pillow, squinted blearily at the morning light just dusting in through the window, then glared at the phone as it shrieked at her again.

Her eyes felt gritty from lack of sleep, and her mind was still sorting through the hundred or so different emotions she'd experienced since Dan had walked out her door without a backward glance.

She flinched slightly just remembering the quiet snick of the lock closing and the terrible emptiness of the house when he'd gone. She'd hurt him. Damn it, she knew she'd hurt him, and she hadn't meant to. But the flicker of pain in his eyes had been unmistakable. Though no one else would likely have seen it. Marines apparently were trained to hide the pain. Or maybe it was just Dan's way of defending…protecting himself. Much as she was trying to do.

And now he'd walked away. To protect her.

She scraped one hand across her eyes and wondered how this had all gotten out of hand so quickly.

When the phone rang for the fourth time, she answered it just to make it be quiet. How could a woman torture herself with all this noise?

"Hello?" she demanded when she picked up the receiver.

"Well, a happy good-morning to you, too," a familiar voice responded.

"Oh," Angela said, pushing herself up against the pillows and shoving her hair back from her face. "It's you."

"I see you missed me," her sister Marie said on a laugh. "What a warm and touching greeting."

Okay, Marie didn't deserve to have her head snapped off. Since she'd become pregnant, the woman had been practically vibrating with happiness. Ordinarily it wasn't this hard to take.

"Sure I did," Angela managed to say, glancing at the bedside clock and realizing she had a few minutes to talk before getting Jeremy up and moving. "But you're just back from vacation. Why are you up at the crack of dawn?"

"Cars are stacking up at the garage," Marie said. "Gotta get busy while I can still get my stomach close enough to a car to work on it."

Despite the sleepless night and the still-unresolved feelings about Dan, Angela found herself smiling. "And how is our baby today?"

"Growing," Marie said, laughing gently. "I swear, Ange, this kid is gonna be huge by the time I'm ready to deliver."

Instantly a wash of memories swept over her. She recalled vividly every kick, every move Jeremy had made while she'd carried him. And how she'd enjoyed it. She'd been young enough then to believe that Bill would get accustomed to marriage. That he would want more children with her.

An old ache throbbed inside her.

"Angela?"

"Hmm?"

"What's wrong?" Marie asked. Then worry colored her tone, as she demanded, "Is it Jeremy? Is he all right?"

"Yeah," she said quickly, hurrying to reassure her sister. "Jeremy's fine."

"Then what is it? You don't sound right."

"It's early. You woke me up."

"That's not it and you know it."

"Let it go, Marie."

"Not a chance," her sister told her. "Tell you

what. I'll meet you at Little League practice this afternoon. We'll talk.''

"Marie—" Angela nearly shouted, but it was too late. The other woman had already hung up.

Well, perfect, she thought. Now she'd have to explain to Jeremy why Dan hadn't shown up at practice—since she knew he wouldn't after last night. And she'd have the extra added joy of being grilled by her little sister.

When a day starts out this good, she thought on a groan, there's nowhere to go but up.

"Why won't he be there?" Jeremy demanded. "He's my coach!"

"He's *one* of your coaches, honey," she said as she steered the car into the parking lot. "Joe will still be here."

Jeremy chewed at his bottom lip and turned his face to stare out the windshield. She felt his hurt, his disappointment, and there wasn't a darn thing she could do about it.

"He promised to show me how to play catcher," Jeremy whispered in a strained voice that seemed to scrape along Angela's spine.

Her throat tightened, and she asked herself again, as she had all day, if she'd done the right thing in letting Dan walk out of her life. Did she really have the right to deprive her son of the friendship of a man he obviously admired?

Too late, she told herself. Too late to back out

now. The deed was done. Dan was gone. They would just have to get by without him. They'd been fine before Dan Mahoney; surely they'd be fine after him, too. But she had to wonder—was she in danger of doing to Jeremy what Dan's mother had obviously done to him? Would her fears make it impossible for her son to find happiness when he was grown? Had she cheated them both out of a chance at happiness?

"Mo-om," Jeremy said impatiently. "What about him teaching me how to be catcher?"

She sighed. "Your aunt Marie used to play catcher on her high school team," she said, hoping to win even a small smile from the stoic boy beside her.

"Aunt Marie's cool, but she's still a girl," he muttered, dipping his head until his expression was hidden in the shadow of the brim of his cap. "Besides," he added, running the back of his hand under his nose, "she's gonna have a baby now. She can't catch."

Angela sighed, pulled into a parking space, set the gearshift to Park and turned off the engine. Taking off her seat belt, she shifted on the seat until she was facing her son. Then, reaching out, she tipped his chin up and looked at him. "Honey, Dan's busy. He's a Marine. He has things he has to do."

She felt awful. Making up excuses about Dan when all the time it was *her* fault her son was hurting. If Dan hadn't been worried about what lay between them, he would be here today, waiting to teach her son more of the mysteries of baseball.

"He promised," Jeremy said stubbornly.

"I know, honey." Dan's words from the night before rang in her ears. What he'd said about being a boy and having promises broken almost before they'd been made. "But sometimes, no matter how badly we want to keep our promises, we just can't. Things happen."

"Yeah, I know," Jeremy said, shooting his mother a quick look. "When I'm grown-up I'll understand."

He opened the car door, got out and slammed it shut again. Sighing, Angela got out, too, and followed after him as he walked to the field. The boy walked with his head hanging and his shoulders bowed. And every plodding step he took was like an arrow of guilt into Angela's heart.

It was as if he knew she was to blame for bursting his bubble and was really making her pay. Geez. She'd only wanted to protect him. Keep him from being disappointed. Yet here he was, looking as though his world had ended.

So what had she accomplished? Nothing.

"Hey!"

She grappled her way out of her black thoughts to focus on Jeremy. "What is it?"

He turned around, flashed her the grin she knew

so well and pointed off into the distance. "Look! It's Dan. He *did* come!"

"What?" She shifted her gaze to the baseball field and blinked and looked again just to be sure of what she was seeing. But it was real. There stood Dan Mahoney, leaning casually against the bleachers, talking and laughing with Marie. As if nothing was wrong. As if nothing at all had happened last night.

She couldn't believe it. He'd actually kept his word to her son despite how things had been left between them. A small spot of warmth settled into the cold ring around her heart.

"I told you," Jeremy said on a victorious laugh, "I told you Dan wouldn't break his promise!" Then he turned and raced off across the grass toward his hero.

Dan turned from Marie to watch Jeremy running toward him, and despite his nagging headache and the uncertain swirl of emotions inside him, he smiled.

"Dan!" the boy shouted. "I knew you'd come."

"Why wouldn't I?" he asked, lifting his gaze to briefly rest on Angela.

"Don't I get a hello?" Marie asked, and held out her arms for a hug.

"Sure," Jeremy said, obliging her quickly so the fellas wouldn't see him actually hugging a girl. "Dan's my coach," he told her as he stepped back.

"So he says. Is he a good one?"

Jeremy paused before saying, "Not as good as you."

She laughed and slapped his hat brim. "Smart kid, that's what you are."

Dan hardly heard the byplay. All he could see was Angela. All he could think was how hard this would be. Seeing her all the time and being unable to have her.

Then Jeremy tugged at his T-shirt, and Dan looked down into brown eyes so much like hers.

"Mom said you couldn't be coach anymore. She said you were too busy."

Shifting his gaze to Angela's again, he saw surprise in her eyes. She really hadn't expected him to show up. "I'm never too busy to keep a promise," he told the boy even while his gaze bored into Angela's. She flushed a little, and he knew his barb had hit home.

"That's what *I* told her," Jeremy said, shaking his head.

Angela was still staring at him and Dan had to force himself to look away. What he wanted to do was grab her, kiss her senseless, then find the closest patch of grass and lay her down on it. Everything in him tightened until he felt as if even breathing was a monumental task. But he'd done the right thing last night. It was painful. But pain he knew. Pain he could deal with.

Best to forget about Angela and concentrate on what he owed to the kid.

Looking at Jeremy, he said, "How about we go throw the ball around a little until the rest of the team gets here?"

"Yeah," the kid said eagerly, "and will you show me how to throw a curveball?"

"Not until you're older," Dan said, already turning the boy toward the diamond. "You'll throw out your elbow."

"Oh," he said solemnly. "See, that's the kind of stuff girls don't know."

Dan smiled, looked up at Marie. "Nice to see you again."

"Likewise," she said.

Then he followed Jeremy to the field. His smile gone, he nodded to Angela in a polite but less-than-friendly gesture as he passed her.

Angela winced. He couldn't have made himself any clearer. He was here strictly for her son's sake. Which was a good thing, right? She looked over her shoulder at the two of them and heard herself sigh before she turned and climbed up onto the bleachers. Taking a seat beside her sister, she propped her elbows on her knees and cupped her chin in her hands.

"So what was that all about?" Marie asked.

"It's a long story."

Marie reached out and gave her a pat on the back. "Then you'd better get started."

Well, she'd been expecting that. There wasn't a Santini alive who wouldn't demand the details.

A half hour later Marie nodded and looked off at the man leading sliding exercises. "So. What we have here is a terrific man who likes you—"

"Liked," Angela corrected. "Past tense."

"Uh-huh," Marie said, then went on, "and likes your son enough to give up what rare free time he has to be a Little League coach." Turning her head to look at her sister, she smirked and said, "Yeah, there's a real creep."

The wind shot unimpeded across the field, tugging at her hair, stinging her eyes. Angela shrugged deeper into the folds of her sweatshirt and tried to think of the right thing to say. Tried to find the words to defend a position she knew was already crumbling.

"You don't understand," Angela started, but her sister cut her off again. Honestly, she'd forgotten how pushy Marie could be.

"I know, Bill was a jerk."

"I never said that," Angela said, sitting up straight and shaking her head. At least, she hadn't said it out loud. "He was Jeremy's father—I would never say that."

"Maybe not," Marie admitted, "but *we* all did."

"Thanks very much."

"Don't get sniffy. You know darn well it's the truth."

"And the truth is always so easy to hear," she said, sarcasm dripping from every word.

"And lying is so much better."

She opened her mouth to speak, then thought better of it and closed it again.

Marie rubbed her rounded belly thoughtfully as she spoke, "Ange, you've been living like a nun for three years."

"Yeah," Angela pointed out, "and the first time I cut loose, look what happens." She shook her head again. "Nope, back to the cloister for me."

"Oh, that's brilliant," her sister snapped.

"Well, what else can I do?"

Marie looked at her as if she had horns growing out of her head. "Take a chance, for Pete's sake. Live a little. He seems like a perfectly nice guy...."

"...who told me the first night we met he wasn't looking for a relationship, either."

"Things change," Marie said, glancing down at the mound of the child she carried within her. "A few months ago I didn't know Davis Garvey existed," she said thoughtfully. "Now I love him more than I ever thought it possible to love anyone, and I'm pregnant with his baby."

Angela sighed, reached out a hand and laid it gently atop Marie's belly. "And I'm happy for you, honey. But it's different for me. I have Jeremy to think about."

"Yeah, you do," she said, and waved one hand to indicate the boy out on the field. "And look at him. He's in seventh heaven out there. He's nuts about Dan.''

"I know," Angela said on a moan. "That's what makes this so hard."

"No," Marie countered. "*You're* what's making it so hard. Honestly, Ange, if somebody handed you a million bucks, you'd tell them no thanks if the bills weren't folded right."

"That's not fair."

"Maybe not, but it's accurate."

"You don't know—"

"I do, though. I see it in your eyes." Marie shifted her gaze to follow Angela's. "When you watch him, a light comes on inside. Like you're glowing or something."

"Maybe your glow is rubbing off," she said, making a halfhearted attempt to argue.

"Pregnancy isn't contagious," Marie said, then paused and asked, "Or could it be…?"

Oh, yeah. That's just what she'd need about now. Another complication. Although a part of her still hungered for more children, she knew darn well she was in no position to end up pregnant.

"I'm not stupid, Marie," Angela said, stiffening her spine. "We were careful."

"Well, good," Marie said. "At least, I think that's good. I mean, at least if you got pregnant, you'd have to talk to the man."

"Oh," Angela said, appalled. "Great plan. Get

pregnant to start a conversation. Honestly, I thought Gina was the ditzy sister.''

Marie laughed, and Angela scowled at her. ''Gina is no longer the ditz in the family. Just ask her new—and probably still-doting—husband.''

''When do they get back from their honeymoon?'' Angela asked innocently, in an attempt to change the subject.

''Saturday night as you well know,'' Marie said. ''I know what you're trying to do, and I'm not finished talking about your First Sergeant.''

''He's not mine, and I am finished.''

''Touchy, touchy,'' Marie tsked.

Angela tipped her face up toward the sky. ''Why wasn't I an only child?''

Marie gave her a punch in the arm. ''Just lucky, I guess.''

''Yeah, I guess,'' Angela admitted, sliding one arm around her sister's shoulders. Truth was, she couldn't imagine her life without Marie and Gina in it. Although, at the moment she could do with a little less family interference.

''Well,'' her sister said slowly, shooting that wish down the tubes, ''now that you're feeling all friendly toward me again, I have a question.''

''Just one?''

Flicking a quick look out at Dan, she said, ''You have to tell me something about your magic weekend.''

"What?" she asked, giving her sister a wary glance.

"How good was it?"

Good? What a small word. Instantly images flashed across her mind. Dan's hands, his mouth, his tongue. Her body lifting into his, arching. His body sliding into hers, claiming her, taking her to heights she hadn't expected, only to go still higher.

Her heartbeat quickened, her mouth went dry, and if she hadn't been sitting down, she was fairly certain her knees would have given out on her. Heat pooled at her center, and she shifted uncomfortably on the bleachers.

"Wow," Marie whispered.

"What?" Angela asked, "I didn't even answer your question yet."

Marie looked at her sister's flushed face and the sparkle in her eyes and smiled to herself. "Oh, Ange, you answered it all right."

A few days later Mama was home and planning a big family dinner to celebrate everyone being together again. The kitchen smelled wonderful, and the windows steamed with the thick fog brought on by boiling pasta. At least *this* part of Angela's life was back to normal.

The past few days had been awful. Seeing Dan at the baseball field, watching him draw closer to her son while at the same time drawing farther away from her.

But this is what she wanted, right? She wanted to be safe. Protected from ever making the kind of mistake she'd made with Bill. She'd wanted her heart safe. So now it was. But it was also so empty.

"Angela," Mama said, "Pay attention now. Gina and Nick will be here and Marie and Davis of course."

Angela nodded over the grocery list, barely listening to Mama count off family members. Why bother? she thought. We all know how many of us there are.

"Then there's you and me and Jeremy and Dan..."

Whoa.

"Excuse me?" Angela dropped the pen onto the kitchen table and stared at her mother. "Who did you say?"

"You, me, Jeremy and Dan."

"That's the one," she said and stood up. She couldn't believe this. "Dan? Why are you inviting Dan to a family dinner?"

"Jeremy asked me to," her mother said, clearly surprised by Angela's reaction.

"Well, uninvite him."

"I will not," Mama said, folding her arms across her middle. "Jeremy asked him yesterday at practice, and Dan accepted. He's coming."

"Nobody told me." What was going on here? A conspiracy?

"I'm sorry, honey, I didn't know I had to clear things with you first."

Sometimes her mother did sarcasm better than Marie.

But Angela wasn't ready to give in yet. For heaven's sake, wasn't it bad enough that she and Dan were busily ignoring each other on a baseball field? Did they *have* to do it at the dinner table, too? "You invited a *stranger* to dinner?"

One of Mama's brows lifted, a sure sign of growing displeasure. Angela ignored it and said, "You don't even know him!"

"He's not a stranger," her mother said firmly. "He's Jeremy's coach, and he's a friend of Nick's. He was in the wedding. You met him."

Did she ever, she thought, and wondered if her mother would still be so set on inviting Dan to dinner if she knew exactly how well the man knew one of her daughters.

"Is there something you're not telling me?" Mama asked.

"No," Angela said quickly, too quickly, and lowered her gaze. "Nothing." No way was she going to admit to a red-hot affair to her mother. And there was no other way out of this. So it appeared she was stuck. Still, she made one last try. "If you want to invite some man we hardly know to a family dinner, where he'll probably be very uncomfortable, then that's your business."

"Well, thank you, honey," her mother said. "I appreciate your confidence in my judgment."

"Very funny."

"I thought so."

Frowning, Angela scooped up the grocery list and swung her purse up onto her shoulder. "I'll be back in an hour or so."

"I'll be here," Mama said, already turning back to the stove. "Well, at least until about six."

Angela stopped on the way to the door. "What's at six?"

Her mother waved one hand over her head and turned away. "I'm going out to dinner," she said. "This pasta is for you and Jeremy."

"Out to dinner? Oh. Are you and Margaret going out to reminisce about the cruise?"

"Hmmm..."

Angela shook her head at that nonanswer and plucked her car keys from the key ring by the door. Then she headed out to the driveway, wondering why even her mother seemed a little...different, somehow.

What had happened to her pleasant little cloistered world?

Eleven

As family dinners went, it was pretty good.

Dan stood in one corner of the living room, letting his gaze drift across the small cluster of people gathered there. Jeremy, the Santini women and the two Marines who'd married into this family, looked comfortable, easy with each other, and Dan envied them even as he felt more than ever like the outsider he was.

Hell, he wasn't even sure why he'd accepted Jeremy's invitation. But even as that thought flitted through his mind, he recognized it for the lie it was. His gaze slipped to the one woman he hadn't been able to stop thinking about all week. He'd come to see her, because seeing her at a distance at baseball practice wasn't enough. But maybe it had been a mistake to come.

Here, in the heart of her family, she seemed even more distant from him than ever.

"That's a very serious face, Sergeant," a voice from close by said.

He swiveled his head to look down into Maryann Santini's big brown eyes. "Just thinking, ma'am."

She nodded thoughtfully and looked across the room at her oldest daughter. "Thinking what, I wonder?" Then, shifting her gaze back to him, she said, "Mahoney, that's Irish, isn't it?"

"Yes, ma'am, it is," he said, wondering where she was going with this line of questioning.

"So, not Italian," she mused, then asked, "Are you Catholic?"

"Used to be," he said, remembering all of the masses he'd attended as a boy. It had been a long time since he'd been inside a church, though. He took a firmer grip on his bottle of beer, cleared his throat and asked a question of his own. "Does that matter?"

"Not really, I suppose," Maryann said, giving his arm a gentle pat. "My grandson tells me you're a nice man, and that's the most important thing."

Nice. Well, it had been a lot of years since anyone had accused him of being *nice*. Still, it felt pretty good to know that at least he had *one* fan in this room. But he had the distinct impression Mrs.

Santini wasn't asking these questions without a plan in mind.

As she went on, telling him about her family, and Angela specifically, he let his gaze drift again, back to the woman whose image never seemed to leave his mind.

"Has anyone got a hose?" Gina asked no one in particular.

Her husband, Nick, came up behind her, encircled her neck and shoulders with one arm and drew her back against him. "Planning a water fight?" he asked, dipping his head to plant a quick kiss on her cheek.

"Nope," she said, reaching up to lay one hand on his muscular forearm, "planning to hose down my sister and the man setting fire to her with his eyes."

"Huh?"

"You noticed, too," Marie said as she came up beside her younger sister.

"Noticed?" Gina said with a soft laugh. "A blind man would notice."

"Notice what?" Marie's husband, Davis, asked as he joined them.

"Just what I was going to ask," Nick said.

"Correction," Gina said with a slow shake of her head. "A blind *woman* would notice."

"Have you had your eyesight checked lately,

Marine?'' Marie asked her husband as she threaded her arm through his.

"Tell me what I'm looking at, and I'll tell you if I see it." He let one hand drop to absentmindedly rub the swollen curve of her belly, and she moved into his touch.

"Okay, you guys," Marie said, looking from her husband to Nick. "Take a look at Dan, then at Angela. Now, pay close attention to the lightning crackling in the air and the smoke rising from the top of Dan's head."

"What're you talking about?" Nick asked, straightening up slightly.

Gina tipped her head back to look at her husband fondly. "Honestly, honey, she's talking about how Dan is right now stripping my sister naked with his eyes."

"Hmmm..." Davis murmured, narrowing his gaze to look back and forth between the couple under observation.

"What's going on here?" Nick demanded.

"Looks to me like we've got another Santini woman lining up to take the fall," Gina said with a small laugh.

"Yeah, well," her husband said, "remember I told you to warn her about Dan at the wedding? He's not a commitment kind of guy."

Marie and Gina exchanged glances and laughed together briefly. Then Marie spoke up. "Nick, were you looking to get married when you met Gina?"

He scowled at her.

"Nope," Gina answered for him. "As I recall, all he wanted was to learn how to—"

"Cook," Nick finished for her, still not wanting to talk about the whole dance class thing.

"Right," his new wife said with a knowing smile.

"What's your mother doing?" Davis asked, as he watched the older woman talking to Dan.

"My guess?" Marie asked. "I'm thinking she started out with the first few questions she asked you, sweetie. Are you Italian? Are you Catholic?"

"Oh man…" Sympathy colored Davis's voice as he shook his head in memory. "She's shopping for another son-in-law."

"Dan?" Nick scoffed at the idea. "Not a chance."

"Stranger things have happened," Gina whispered, and Nick had to agree. But still, he was going to be having a little chat with his old friend.

Angela shifted uncomfortably on the couch. This was probably going to be the longest night of her life. Sitting here, in the middle of her family, with a man who knew her body more intimately than anyone ever had before.

She flicked another glance at him and caught him staring at her. Her blood actually boiled in her veins. That was the only explanation for the sudden and overwhelming surge of heat that swamped her from head to toe. The air seemed too thick to breathe, and her heart was pounding so loudly in her ears she couldn't even hear the hum of conversations around her.

Distract yourself, her brain silently ordered. Think of something else. *Anything* else. Her gaze slid to her mother's animated features. *What is Mama saying to him?* Oh, yeah, that should be enough to worry anybody. As she watched, Jeremy walked to Dan's side and casually wrapped one arm around the man's waist.

Angela's heartbeat staggered as Dan absentmindedly dropped his arm around the boy's shoulder and tugged him close for a brief, hard hug. Never before, she realized, feeling the sting of tears crowd her eyes, never before had Jeremy so casually offered affection to a man. His father hadn't been interested in his son, and Jeremy had learned that quickly enough. Lately he'd enjoyed Nick's and Davis's company, but clearly, her son had bonded big-time with Dan.

Even though his own father had hurt him, disappointed him, Jeremy had taken a risk. He'd obviously given his heart to the Marine who'd invaded their lives. Lord, her little boy made her feel like a coward.

She looked at Dan again and wondered if she was making a mistake by running from what she was feeling. Strong, kind, passionate, he was a man most women dreamed of finding. But could she really trust another man not to hurt her? Not to hurt Jeremy? Wasn't it better, safer, to stay locked away in a small, insular world, than to risk the pain of losing again?

In Dan's eyes she read the same longing, the same confusion she knew was in her own. And a part of her wanted to walk over to him and join the small unit he and her son made. But because that want was suddenly so strong, she left the room, instead, to go into the kitchen and check on dinner.

"Okay," Dan said as he walked into the dark garage, "what's so important it couldn't wait until tomorrow at the base?"

Nick hit the wall switch, and a long bank of fluorescent lights flickered into life.

One look into the other man's eyes had Dan wondering if maybe he shouldn't be looking for a place to hide. But he had never run from anything in his life, and he damned sure wouldn't start by running from a friend.

"What the hell do you think you're doing?" Nick demanded in a harsh whisper.

Folding his arms across his chest, Dan planted his feet in a wide stance, narrowed his eyes and said, "Well now, that depends on what you're talking about."

He stabbed the air with his index finger, pointing at the house. "I'm talking about Angela."

Dan pulled in a long, deep breath. No way was he going to apologize for Angela.

"She's my *family* now, damn it," Nick was saying, "and nobody messes with my family. Not even you."

Nice to know what your "friends" think of you. Taking a step toward him, Dan spoke through gritted teeth. "Is that what you think I was doing? Just killing a little time?"

Nick snorted a laugh and shook his head. "We both know your reputation, Dan."

All right, maybe he deserved that. Scrubbing one hand across his face, he looked at the other man and met his gaze squarely. "This was different."

"Yeah?" he asked, unconvinced. "How?"

How indeed. Hell, he didn't know. He hardly knew whether he was coming or going lately. Shaking his head, he could only say, "It doesn't really matter now, anyway. It's over."

"Doesn't look that way to me," Nick said, and his tone was less belligerent now.

Dan would rather face anger than sympathy, so he turned his head to stare at the house. Squares of light spilled onto the dark driveway, and he could hear snatches of female laughter from inside. Behind the curtains people moved, doing simple things like fixing a meal, talking, gathering together.

And for the first time in his life, Dan Mahoney wanted to belong. He wanted to know he was a part of their world. He ached to be included in the easy laughter and the comfortable conversations. He desperately wanted to be in the warmth of that house, with Angela and Jeremy beside him. He wanted— no, *needed*—that woman more than he needed his next breath.

And he couldn't have her.

"I don't believe it," Nick said as he came up beside him.

"What now?" Dan asked, never taking his gaze from the lit windows.

"Dan Mahoney, king of the one-night stands, in love."

"Shut up. Nobody said anything about love."

Nick laughed shortly and slapped him on the back. "Welcome to the family, man!"

Dan shrugged his friend's hand off and shook his head. "I told you. It's over."

"Why?" Nick asked, his tone getting suspiciously ugly again. "Not interested in a ready-made family?"

"That's not it, damn it," Dan snapped, turning on Nick with a vengeance. "A man'd have to be crazy not to want a kid like Jeremy for a son."

"Then what's your problem?"

"Right now?" Dan asked. "You. Why don't you just butt the hell out?"

"I already told you why. She's family."

"So fine," Dan snapped. "You did your duty. I told you it's over. After tonight I'll stay clear." He held up one hand. "Clear of Angela. I promised Jeremy to coach his team, and that's just what I'm gonna do, whether you like it or not."

"Is that right?"

"That's right, *Gunny.*" That should do it, he thought. Remind the man that Dan outranked him and he was walking a fine line here. Sure they were friends. But he wasn't going to put up with this much longer, and Nick had better realize that.

"Gonna pull rank on me?" the other man asked. "That's a cowardly way to win an argument, *First Sergeant.*"

"Fine," Dan said. "Leaving rank out of this, you should still back off."

A long minute passed in tense silence before Nick finally said, "I've got to say, you surprise me."

"How's that?" Dan asked, not really caring.

"I've never seen you quit before."

Dan drew in a long, deep breath and blew it out again. It'd be a shame to wreck this garage in a fistfight, but if that's the way Nick wanted it... "Man, I'm in no mood for this. And since we're leaving rank out of this, unless you're looking for a black eye, I'd advise you to drop it. Now."

"You'll fight me, but you'll walk away from Angela?"

"I'm telling you, Nick—"

The man shook his head. "It doesn't make sense. I mean, I've seen you dog tired and still running.

I've seen you drag an unconscious man out of harm's way, never considering your own danger. I've seen you—"

"I get it," Dan snapped, interrupting the long list of past accomplishments. "You've seen me."

"What I don't get is why you're so ready to walk away from a Santini woman. Let me tell you something…they're worth the trouble." Nick smiled, but Dan didn't return it. His friend meant well, but he didn't understand how it was.

"I don't want to hurt her," Dan admitted, not sure why he'd said it aloud. Hell, maybe he wanted someone to tell him he was doing the right thing. He shifted his gaze from his friend back to the house where Angela waited inside.

"Judging from what my wife and her sister tell me, your leaving has already hurt her."

"She wasn't interested in anything longer than a weekend."

"Doesn't sound like Angela to me," Nick growled.

No, it didn't. Did she care? He wondered. He would like to think he mattered to her as much as she did to him. But even then, it wouldn't change anything. "It's better a small pain now than a bigger one later."

"And what makes you so damn sure you'd hurt her?"

Dan inhaled sharply and blew it out in a rush. "Because I'm my old man's son," he said flatly.

"Hell, even my own mother predicted that I'd grow up to make some woman miserable. My old man's leaving nearly killed my mother. I won't do that to Angela."

Nick walked a few steps until he was standing right in front of Dan. "So, what you're thinking is…I'll marry her, then I'll leave her."

"I didn't say that."

"And you figure Angela's such a weakling she'd fall apart and never be the same again?"

"Angela's no weakling," he said, arguing that point. His mother had gone from one man to the next, always looking for someone to save her. Rescue her. Angela would save herself. "She's a helluva lot stronger than some of the Marines on base. She's raising a terrific kid. On her own. She's a teacher. She's funny. Warm. Generous."

"But you don't love her or anything."

Dan slid a glance at him. "Who're you? Dear Abby?"

Nick laughed aloud and clapped one hand down hard on Dan's shoulder. "Don't you get it, you moron? If you're this worried about hurting her—and Jeremy—you're not the man your father was."

A tiny, tiny speck of light appeared in the cold emptiness of his heart.

"Geez, Marine." Shaking his head, Nick turned for a look at the house. "Have you *ever* quit on anything or anybody?"

No, he thought, he never had.

"And," Nick said, adding fuel to the fire in Dan's brain, "has anything in your life been as important to you as Angela?"

"No," he said it aloud this time and felt that small speck of light burn brighter, stronger. Nick was right, he thought, and wondered why he'd never seen it himself. He wasn't a quitter. He would never walk away from something important to him.

"Then what the hell's your problem?"

The problem, he thought, was he'd spent most of his life worrying about something that didn't *have* to happen. He could be the man he wanted to be. Not the one he might have been born to be. A slow dawning blossomed inside him, and for the first time in days he pulled in an easy breath. Suddenly possibilities opened up in front of him, and he found himself actually hoping that he and Angela could find a future together.

Dan laughed shortly as his thoughts whirled. "Besides a nosy friend?"

"Man, until you marry into the Santini clan, you have no idea what nosy really is." He twisted the gold ring on his finger and smiled to himself. "These women know everything you're thinking and feeling and never let you get away with a damn thing."

"And you're lovin' it."

"Damn straight," Nick said with a grin. "You're gonna fit right in."

"Oo-rah," Dan muttered, and told himself that

all he had to do now was let go of a lifetime of fears and take a chance on love.

No problem.

"He's a nice man," Mama said, giving the sauce another stir with a long handled wooden spoon. "I like him."

"Well," Angela said tightly, "that's a relief."

"I like him, too," Gina piped up. "He's cute."

"Always important," Angela muttered, setting out knives and forks beside the plates.

"He's a friend of Nick's so he must be all right," Marie added her two cents worth.

"Well what're you waiting for? Book the church," Angela told her.

Both sisters gave her a look that clearly said they thought she was crazy. But it didn't matter what they thought, did it? They hadn't been married to Bill. They hadn't seen hopes and dreams and love die a slow death from neglect and disinterest.

Mama tapped excess sauce off the spoon and set it down. Turning around to face her oldest daughter, she ignored the other two, planted both hands on her hips and demanded, "What's wrong with him, then? You don't find him attractive?"

Attractive? Let's see. Did the fact that all she could think about was using her teeth to tear off his shirt count? Heat surged through her, and she had to take a breath before saying as casually as she could manage, "Of course I find him attractive."

Gina snorted.

Angela scowled at her. Gina's hormones had *always* been on overdrive.

"He's good with Jeremy," Mama said.

"Jeremy's nuts about him," Angela admitted sourly.

"The way you look at him I'm surprised he doesn't burst into flames."

"Mama!" Angela said on a surprised gasp. Even her sisters were stunned.

Maryann Santini looked from one to the other of them before clucking her tongue in disgust. "What? You think I was *born* fifty years old? I don't know what desire is? I don't know how it feels to want someone so badly you want to weep for it?"

"Oh," Angela mumbled, pulling out a chair and sinking into it, "this just can't get any weirder."

"Honey," Mama said as she walked to her side and laid one hand on her shoulder, "life is hard enough. Don't turn your back on love when you stumble across it. Love's a gift. It's what makes everything worthwhile."

She would like to believe that. But she'd learned the hard way that love wasn't always an answer. Besides, "This can't be love," she whispered, more to herself than to any of the others, "I've only known him a couple of weeks."

"Bull," Mama said and pulled a chair out to sit down beside Angela.

"Bull?" she echoed with a laugh. Mama was full of surprises tonight.

"Love doesn't run on a calendar, Angela," Mama said, taking her daughter's hand in hers. "I knew your papa, God rest him, ten days before I agreed to marry him, and I never regretted it. Not for a moment."

"And look at me and Davis," Marie tossed in. "And Gina and Nick."

"Yeah," Gina said wryly, "we're not exactly known for long engagements around here, are we?"

"But I knew Bill for years, and it still went bad," Angela said.

"If anything," Gina said softly, "that should be an endorsement for doing things the quick way."

Angela smiled, but shook her head. "I can't risk it," she said. "Not again. I have Jeremy to think about now."

"Jeremy's important," her mother agreed. "But so are you. If you're miserable, will that make Jeremy happy?"

"No, but..."

"Exactly," Mama said. "No buts."

"It's not that easy," Angela said softly. "I mean, Dan *seems* sincere...."

"Maybe he *is* sincere," Marie said.

Angela looked up into the faces of the women she'd loved all of her life and found herself wondering if they might be right. But even so... "Even if I were willing," she said with a slow shake of her head, "Dan ended it between us a few days ago. He's not interested. Not anymore."

"How come you never come to the house anymore?" Jeremy asked.

"That's a little complicated," Dan answered softly.

Angela held her breath and stood perfectly still. Her son and Dan were standing in the backyard, in the dim glow of the porch light. With everyone gone—even her mother had slipped off to some mysterious "appointment"—Angela had hoped to have a word with Dan. Maybe try to straighten out what was between them. Looked like Jeremy had beaten her to it.

"Doncha like us anymore?" her son asked.

She heard Dan sigh and didn't know if he was pleased or disinterested.

"Sure I do," he said, "but—"

Oh, she thought, a but was never a good sign.

"Then I think you should marry my mom."

Good God. Angela clapped one hand to her forehead. Okay, first her mother, then her son trying to set up a wedding. Could this get any worse? She laughed silently at that. What was she thinking? Of course it could. Dan could say "Thanks but no thanks."

And suddenly Angela knew she didn't want to hear him say it. She knew she didn't want to live the rest of her life without Dan.

She held her breath, cocked her ear toward the open doorway and waited.

"Well, Jeremy," Dan said softly, so softly she almost missed it entirely, "getting married is like making a promise."

"Yeah?"

"And I only make promises I know I can keep."

So what did that mean? she wondered, and scowled to herself as she moved away from the door.

Twelve

Bayside Elementary had been echoing with the shrieks of children for fifty years. The faded, weather-worn pink brick walls were like friendly arms encircling the children, whose laughter and high-pitched voices pierced the air.

At morning recess Angela strolled through the screaming hordes of kids racing across the blacktop out onto the playing fields. A cold spring wind blew in off the ocean, carrying the damp sting of sea salt over the open grounds and buffeted high-flying clouds across a sky so blue it looked like a painting.

Most of the teachers either stayed in their classrooms or huddled together in the teachers' lounge, but Angela needed to be outside. Needed to be moving. Her thoughts raced faster than the hundreds of little feet clattering around her.

"Mrs. Jackson," a little girl shouted, "look at me!"

Angela turned to watch Marci Evans swing from the monkey bars and smiled appropriately. "Wonderful, honey," she called, and kept walking, her mind busy with other things.

Ever since the family dinner two nights ago, she'd been thinking. About her life. Her son. About Dan. Lifting one hand, she rubbed a spot between her eyes, hoping to ease the headache throbbing there. But it didn't help. And not surprising, she thought, since she'd hardly had more than two hours sleep in the last couple of days.

Hard to sleep when the image of Dan's face wouldn't leave her. Hard to sleep while her body burned for his touch and her soul yearned for something she was too afraid to claim. Hard to sleep when her heart ached.

She sighed and let her gaze drift aimlessly across the playground until she spotted a lone child standing beside the chain-link fence surrounding the schoolyard. Jeremy stood, fingers poking through the steel links, his gaze fixed on the parking lot.

Frowning thoughtfully, she walked to him, and when she was close enough, called his name.

He turned his head for a glance at her. Even from a distance she saw the disappointment etched into his features before he returned to his watchful pose, his gaze locked on the parked cars and the street beyond.

"What're you doing?" she asked as she came up beside him and put a hand on his shoulder.

"He didn't come," her son muttered, shaking his head.

"Who didn't come?"

"Dan," Jeremy said tightly, and rested his forehead on the fence. "He said he'd come to Show and Tell today, but it's almost time, and he's not here."

Angela sent a quick look at the parking lot, as if perhaps Jeremy just hadn't seen Dan's car out there. But an instant later she squatted at her son's side, tugging down the hem of her skirt as she did. "Honey," she said, and waited until he looked at her to continue. "It's the middle of the day. I'm sure Dan has work to do on the base."

Jeremy shook his head and bit down hard on his bottom lip to keep it from quivering. "No. He said he'd be here. He said he could. And he's not."

Such a small thing, she thought. No adult would think anything of it. But to a child a disappointment like this was crushing. No doubt Jeremy had told all of his friends about the Marine coming to class, and now he would have to put up with the teasing that would naturally follow Dan's not showing up.

But why wouldn't he come? she asked herself. He'd kept every other promise he'd made to her son. He'd continued to coach Jeremy's Little

League team even after he'd decided to walk away from her. He'd assured them both time and again that he didn't make promises he couldn't keep. There had to be a reason for this, she thought, and surprised herself at her faith in the man.

Somehow, in the past couple of weeks, Dan Mahoney had taught her how to trust again. He'd proven himself to her. He'd proven his loyalty to her son. He'd shown her that he was an honorable man.

The tight pain she'd been carrying around her heart for days lightened a little, and a small, thoughtful smile curved her mouth as she reached out for the small boy standing brokenhearted in front of her. Turning him around to face her, she held his hands in hers and looked deeply into his eyes.

"Dan promised he would be here, right?"

"Uh-huh," he said, and sniffed.

"Then he *will* be," she said firmly.

"But—"

"No buts," she said, and realized with an inward laugh just how much she sounded like her mother. "Dan made a promise and he *always* keeps his promises, doesn't he?"

"Yeah…" He sounded unconvinced, but hopeful.

"Then he'll be here," she said.

"You think?"

She shook her head. "I *know,* and so will you if you think about it."

He sniffed again, furrowed his brow as he considered her words and then finally nodded. "You're right, Mom. He will be here."

Giving his hands one last squeeze, she stood up, and her son, risking personal humiliation, stepped close enough to give her a hard, tight hug. Then he looked up at her, grinned and took off for the playground, obviously no longer feeling the need to stand guard at the fence.

She watched him, then glanced back at the parking lot. "He'll be here," she said aloud, marveling at the ring of confidence in her voice. How could she not have seen it before? How could she not have realized that Dan Mahoney was a man to be trusted? A man to whom honor was everything? A man who would be the kind of husband she'd always dreamed of. A man who would be the father Jeremy so deserved. A man she would love forever.

"Show and Tell, huh?" she whispered as she started walking back toward the school. When he was finished with Jeremy's class, maybe she would just intercept the First Sergeant on his way out of school and "show and tell" *him* a few things.

A half hour later Angela was at the chalkboard, writing down a few math problems, when she heard an unfamiliar sound. She paused, holding the piece of chalk away from the slate and cocked her head to listen again.

With her classroom door open to the quiet hallways, the rhythmic *click* of sound grew louder as it came nearer. Setting the chalk down into its tray, she stepped out from behind her desk and waved a distracted hand at her class to keep them quiet. Then she walked to the doorway and looked out.

"Oh, my goodness..." she murmured, astonished.

Marching down the middle of the hallway was the most spit-and-polished Marine she had ever seen. He looked like a recruitment poster. Wearing his Dress Blue uniform, complete with sword, Dan Mahoney moved with a stiff spine precision usually reserved for a parade ground. At his side was a grinning, wide-eyed Jeremy, and directly behind the pair were smiling women from the office and a few of the teachers whose rooms he'd already passed.

Angela's mouth went dry and her stomach did a quick pitch and roll. He wasn't doing all of *this* for a second-grade Show and Tell class. There was more here. Much more. Backing up into her classroom, she ignored the rumble of curiosity from the third-graders at their desks. With her gaze locked on the open doorway, she tried to concentrate on breathing, and found it increasingly difficult as the seconds ticked past. She kept backing up until she bumped into the edge of her desk.

And in that instant Dan did a sharp, right-face

turn, clicking his heels for emphasis before striding
into her room and crossing the space between them.
Absently she heard her class's combined intake of
breath, and wished she could draw one herself.

"You were right, Mom," Jeremy crowed, and
his sweet voice was no more than a buzzing in her
ears. "Dan came, just like you said he would. And
he took me out of my room 'cause he said I had to
be here when he talked to you." With that, her son
turned a superior look at the older kids staring at
him with envy.

"I hope you don't mind, Mrs. Jackson," Jeremy's teacher said from behind Dan, "but I thought
it best if I accompanied Jeremy…"

Uh-huh. It wasn't fear for the boy's safety that
had prompted Donna Jarvis's presence. It was simple curiosity.

But Angela didn't care. In fact, except for her
son, the room might have been empty of anyone
but Dan and her.

She stared at him, silently commanding her flut-
tering heart to steady its beat. She watched as he
reached up, removed his pristine-white cover and
tucked it beneath his left arm. Then his gaze met
hers, and she read hope and love and promises in
those beautiful green eyes of his.

"Angela," he said, and his voice boomed out,
creating silence in its wake, "I am your Knight in
Marine Armor."

Oh, my. An inner smile built within, and her knees quaked.

With a flourish he reached across his body with his right hand and drew his ceremonial sword free of its scabbard, the polished steel ringing in tune with a combined gasp of awe from the watching children. The gleaming metal shone in the glitter of sunlight through the windows, and when Dan brought the hilt close to his face, holding the sword pointing straight up into the air, every eye in the room was on him.

Her heart thudded painfully in her chest, and she felt the unmistakable sting of tears at the backs of her eyes.

Then slowly, keeping his back poker straight, Dan went down on one knee in front of her. Angela inhaled sharply, deeply, almost afraid to exhale. Lowering the sword to hold it by his side, he kept his gaze locked with hers as he said loudly, "I want to slay your dragons for you."

One of the teachers in their audience sighed heavily. But Angela wasn't listening. All she heard was Dan's voice saying everything she'd ever wanted to hear.

As if they were alone in the room, he looked only at her, mesmerizing her completely. "I want to be a father to your son and the children we'll have together. I want to love you forever. I want to be the man you love."

"Dan—" She squeezed the single word past the

knot in her throat, and as he slowly stood up she fought for more.

Silently he slid the sword back into its scabbard, then dipped his right hand into the pocket of his tunic. When he withdrew it again and held it out toward her, there was a small, deep-blue velvet box resting in the center of his white-gloved palm.

"Marry me, Angel," he said, his voice softer now, more intimate.

A single tear escaped her eye and rolled un-heeded down her cheek. He blurred in her watery vision and she blinked frantically to clear it.

Reaching out with his left hand, he opened the tiny box to reveal the ring he'd chosen for her. A heart-shaped ruby lay in a cluster of diamonds and winked up at her as if trying to convince her to put it on.

He bent his head toward her and whispered, "It's my heart, Angel. I give it to you. And I promise I will love you forever."

She lifted her gaze from the ring to his eyes. "You promise?" she whispered.

One corner of his mouth tilted in an endearing smile. "I promise. And you know I *always* keep my promises."

"So do I, Marine," she said, and held her left hand out toward him. "And I promise to love you right back."

Something in his eyes sparkled, and he pulled the ring from the box and slid it onto her finger. Then he lifted her hand to his lips and brushed a kiss across her knuckles.

The cool weight of the ring settled on her finger and felt absolutely right.

"We're gettin' married?" Jeremy asked, his voice high and excited.

Dan gave her another smile, then shifted his gaze to the boy who would be his son. "If it's all right with you, we are."

"All right?" Jeremy said laughing, "It was *my* idea!"

Laughing, Dan ruffled his hair. "So it was, son."

Then he turned back to the woman who'd saved him when he didn't even know he needed rescuing. In those soft brown eyes, he saw his future, his happiness and a life he never hoped to have.

"This is some Show and Tell exercise," she whispered as their audience applauded.

"Angel," he murmured, pulling her close, "you ain't seen nothin' yet."

And then he kissed her.

Epilogue

―――――

Three Weeks Later

"**I** now pronounce you husband and wife."

Done, Angela thought. She was a married woman again. And this time she knew it would be good. She felt it right down to her bones. Even her wedding had been perfect this time. No quickie service for Dan Mahoney. It was marriage in a church, in front of their families and friends. It was tradition and honor and all the lovely things she believed in again thanks to this man.

Angela grinned at the priest, then half turned to face her brand-new husband. Already Dan was reaching for her, drawing her close to claim the first kiss of their marriage.

She tilted her head back and looked up into his beautiful pale-green eyes, and read in their depths the happiness she felt singing through her own veins.

"Hello, wife," he murmured.

"Hello, husband," she whispered.

"Did I tell you how beautiful you look today?" His gaze swept her up and down.

"You just did," she answered, and she felt beautiful, in her floor-length, ivory wedding dress with its full skirt, long sleeves and lace around the scooped neck and hem.

"I promise," Dan said as he pulled her closer and bent his head toward hers, "I will love you forever."

"I love you, too," she said softly, and went up on her toes to meet his kiss. His mouth came down on hers gently, reverently and then as seconds ticked past, his arms came hard around her waist, and he deepened the kiss, tipping her backward into a 1930s movie-style dip.

Their audience applauded, the old gray stones of the church ringing with the thunderous sound. When he ended the kiss and set her on her feet again, Angela had to struggle to draw air into suddenly heaving lungs.

Marie, her matron of honor, handed her back the bouquet, and Dan tucked her arm through the crook of his. Together, they looked out at the small sea of smiling faces watching them. As they stood waiting, a short line of Marines, in their Dress-Blues, stood up, turned smartly and marched down the aisle. Their heels clicked musically on the flagstone floor as they continued on outdoors to the front of the church.

Heads turned as everyone shifted to watch. Outside the Marines took their places on either side of the open double doors and, with a choreographed precision, drew their swords and formed an arch of gleaming steel blades that winked and shone in the sunlight.

A knot formed in Angela's throat, and she felt the swift sting of tears fill her eyes.

"Hey!" Jeremy's voice piped up into the suddenly still air.

Blinking, Angela leaned past Dan to look at her son, so tiny, yet so grown-up in his best-man tuxedo.

"What is it, son?" Dan asked, laying one hand on the boy's narrow shoulder.

"Can we have cake now?" Jeremy wanted to know.

Laughter bubbled up around the church, and Dan grinned down at the boy who was now his son. His family. "An excellent idea, Jeremy," he said, then turned back to Angela. "Shall we get this show on the road?"

"Yes, First Sergeant," she said with enthusiasm.

"Then let's do it," he said, and marched her down the aisle. Their friends and family followed quickly after, not wanting to miss their walk through the military archway. Striding beneath the crossed swords, Angela felt Dan's pride in her and the Corps, and something inside her stirred, as well. He'd given her this, too. This feeling of belonging to something bigger than themselves. As they cleared the arch of gleaming steel, the last Marine on the right lowered his sword and gave her behind a swat with the flat of his blade.

"Welcome to the Corps, Mrs. Mahoney," he said, his deep voice carrying above the noise of the gathered crowd.

Angela skittered. Though Dan had warned her ahead of time about this particular tradition, it still caught her off guard. She shot the Marine a look and was in time to see him smile at her. Then, as one, the other Marines called "Ooh-rah!" and sheathed their swords with a single swish of metal.

Their own private color guard broke up then and joined the others surrounding the happy couple. Spring sunshine poured down on them from a deep-blue sky. An ocean wind tugged at her veil, and as their guests swarmed around them, Dan set his hands at her waist and swung her high into the air.

Bracing her hands on his shoulders, Angela looked down into his smiling face and sent a quick, fervent prayer of gratitude heavenward.

"And the last Santini bride bites the dust," Gina said from somewhere close by.

"Last?" Mama asked as Dan set Angela on her feet again. "I don't think so."

"What're you talking about, Mama?" Marie asked over the hubbub of the crowd.

"Only this," their mother said, holding out her left hand to show off a glittering diamond.

"What?" Angela looked from the engagement ring to her mother's beaming face and back again. "What's going on?"

"Salvatore," Maryann Santini called over her shoulder.

Salvatore Mazzeo, a familiar figure in the neighborhood, was a tall, silver-haired man with black eyes, dimples and a string of dry-cleaning stores. He stepped up behind Maryann and dropped a proprietary arm around her shoulders.

"Mama?" Angela said, eyeing her mother suspiciously.

The older woman shrugged, smiled and said simply, "It all started on that cruise. And now Salvatore and I...well, you girls should know that *I'm* going to be the next Santini bride."

As her sisters and their husbands crowded around the engaged couple, Dan pulled a still-surprised Angela to one side.

"Are you upset about your mom?" he asked.

She thought about it for a minute, then shook her head as she looked up at him. "No," she said. "I'm not. I might've been before you and I found each other. But today I want everyone to be as happy as I am.''

He reached up and cupped her cheek in the palm of his hand. ''I'll try to see to it that you're always this happy,'' he said softly, his gaze moving over her face like a caress.

''Just keep loving me,'' she said, ''and I will be.'' Then she turned her face to plant a kiss on his palm.

''I promise,'' he whispered, then winked and gave her a quick grin. ''And you know I *always* keep my promises.''

* * * * *

Look for Maureen Child's next book,
MAROONED WITH A MARINE,
the next installment of the popular
BACHELOR BATTALION *series,*
coming in October
only from Silhouette Desire.

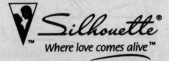

where love comes alive—online...

Visit the *Author's Alcove*

➢ Find the most complete information anywhere on
  your favorite Silhouette author.

➢ Try your hand in the Writing Round Robin—
  contribute a chapter to an online book in the
  making.

Enter the *Reading Room*

➢ Experience an interactive novel—help determine
  the fate of a story being created now by one of
  your favorite authors.

➢ Join one of our reading groups and discuss your
  favorite book.

Drop into *Shop eHarlequin*

➢ Find the latest releases—read an excerpt or write
  a review for this month's Silhouette top sellers.

➢ Try out our amazing search feature—tell us your
  favorite theme, setting or time period and we'll find
  a book that's perfect for you.

All this and more available at

www.eHarlequin.com
on Women.com Networks

COMING NEXT MONTH

#1321 THE DAKOTA MAN—Joan Hohl
Man of the Month
Mitch Grainger always got what he wanted…and what he wanted was his new assistant, Maggie Reynolds. The cunning businessman decided to make Maggie his reward in the ultimate game of seduction…never dreaming *his* heart might become *her* pawn.

#1322 RANCHER'S PROPOSITION—Anne Marie Winston
Body & Soul
All he wanted was a woman to share his ranch—not his bed. But when Lyn Hamill came to work on Cal McCall's South Dakota spread, he began to rethink his intentions. And though Lyn's eyes spoke of a dark past, Cal was determined to make her his wife in every way....

#1323 FIRST COMES LOVE—Elizabeth Bevarly
She'd had a crush on him since she was seven. But it wasn't until her entire hometown suspected Tess Monahan was pregnant that Will Darrow suddenly started showing up at her house offering a helping hand. Now if she could only convince him that she didn't want his hand but his heart....

#1324 FORTUNE'S SECRET CHILD—Shawna Delacorte
Fortune's Children: The Grooms
He thought he would never see Cynthia McCree again. Then suddenly she was back in town—and back in Shane Fortune's life. He had never stopped caring for the vulnerable beauty, but once he discovered the truth about her past, would he still want to make her his Fortune bride?

#1325 MAROONED WITH A MARINE—Maureen Child
Bachelor Battalion
One hurricane, one motel room—and one very sexy Marine—added up to trouble for Karen Beckett. She knew that Gunnery Sergeant Sam Paretti wouldn't leave her alone in the storm. But how did she convince him to stay once the danger had passed…?

#1326 BABY: MacALLISTER-MADE—Joan Elliott Pickart
The Baby Bet
They had one passionate night together, one that best friends Brenda Henderson and Richard MacAllister knew should never be repeated. Then Brenda announced she was pregnant. Now Richard had to convince Brenda that his proposal of marriage was not based on duty…but on love.